THE AVENGERS

Piute was a dusty, sleepy town dozing on the edge of the desert. In the days gone by, its hard-bitten ranchers had made their own law—and the law for horse thieves was a rope. Only Old Man Maxon had cheated them, getting himself shot so his two boys could escape. Since then the town had been real quiet, for quite a few years—the years it took for the Maxon boys to grow up... Now they were home—and the town held its breath in uneasy expectation, watching in the sultry heat, waiting for the bloodbath to erupt.

THE AVENGERS

Chad Merriman

First published in the United States 1959
by Ballantine Books
and in the British Commonwealth 1960
by Transworld

This hardback edition 1998
by Chivers Press
by arrangement with
Golden West Literary Agency

ISBN 0 7540 8015 3

British Library Cataloguing in Publication Data available

Printed and bound in Great Britain by
Redwood Books, Trowbridge, Wiltshire

1

Piute in this obscure light became a ruins: dark, jumbled and lifeless. He knew the impression grew from the fly-by-night buildings and construction shacks sprawling about the cowtown he had remembered so well so long. The star hanging over the far-off desert was the star of morning, which meant daylight would soon bring the place into perspective for what it now was: a rail-head and hell-on-wheels.

He thought it strange that he had awakened at just this hour, which was precisely the hour of a day's dawning when the trouble struck. He wondered if it would be revived now that he and his brother had returned; whether things had endings or if, like day and night, they ran on and on.

He turned away from the window of the hotel room to see his brother Ty stretched on the bed, everything thrown to the foot except the sleazy bottom sheet because the room held so much heat from the day before. He could hear the whistle of Ty's nostrils and wondered why too much drinking dried them out that way. He knew that when he finally did wake up, Ty wouldn't want to go out on the desert that day as they had planned. He would want the hair of the dog, and that would start last night over again.

Zack Maxon began to dress, a tall, hard-shouldered man with a strong, bony face topped raggedly by rusty hair. His motion was lithe, swift and aimed, without hurry or waste. Instead of putting on the suit he had worn on the train coming out from Cheyenne, he rummaged in his sack for work pants and an old blue shirt. When he was dressed in these he felt like himself for the first time in a hard week.

There were sidewalks instead of duckboards and paths

5

in this new Piute, and as the abrupt light of the desert morning pulled the town into focus Zack came onto the walk strung under the board awning of the Nevada Hotel. The railroad edged the site instead of splitting the main street so that the old adobes were still the heart of the place with the new growth sweeping out toward the desert. On the west edge there was the railroad construction camp, dirty tents aflap in the heating wind, heaps of materials and equipment and, still farther off, the contractor's horse camp.

It had not surprised Zack that no one as yet had recognized the Maxon brothers although they had seen men they remembered. It wasn't strange for he had only been fifteen when he left here ten years ago, and Ty two years older. But it was bound to happen and, as his gaze explored the dusty length of the street, it did. Zack felt a sudden worry: the man coming on, tired-looking and dusty, had been closer to him and Ty than anyone on the desert. Then all at once the vague doubts left, and he was glad of this moment.

He saw the advancing rider idly survey him, then the surprise of recognition, and quick slanting of his horse toward Zack.

"You're a Maxon, sure as hell," the man said. "The redhead. You're Zack."

"That's right, Bernie," Zack said, smiling.

Bernie Quick sprang out of the saddle, ducked under the tie rack and held forth a hand. He had the yellow hair, enlarged nose and slightly bucked teeth of the old days, but what had been boyish eyes were now shrewd and hard. As their hands clasped strongly, Zack felt vitality flow from the man, the wild, unruled energy that had made him Ty's friend more than Zack's. They were both full of questions, and Zack got in the first by indirection.

"You must have got up before breakfast to reach town this early."

"Been down to the Comstock," Bernie explained. "Traveled last night to miss the heat. How long are you going to be here, kid? I aimed to get some breakfast and a room and sleep a shift before I went on to the ranch."

"If there's a place open this early," Zack said, "let's go eat now."

6

"Be open by the time I'm ready," Bernie assured him. "This is some town now, Zack. Low life, high life—name it and you can get it right here in sleepy old Piute. Would you have thought that ten years ago?"

"Ten years ago," Zack reflected, "I'd never even seen a railroad, much less guessed there'd be one here, someday."

"Come on while I put up this cayuse."

They tramped along the edge of the sidewalk, Bernie leading the horse, until they came to the Elephant Livery. There Quick turned the animal over to a hostler and ordered it a feed of oats. Afterward he washed at the water trough, then with a proprietary air took Zack to an eating house on the far end of the street.

As they stepped through the doorway Zack suspected why they had come here, for the only one out front was a waitress with frilly black hair, snub nose and shoe-button black eyes. As she came across the floor to the table Bernie took, Zack saw her attractive curves and the provocative, mincing way she walked.

"Hello, Stella," Bernie said. "Who did you keep company with while I was gone?"

"Myself—same as I do when you're in town."

Bernie laughed. "You can get what they call fresh eggs here, Zack, now that there's trains. I'm going to have ham and."

"Suits me," Zack decided.

Stella bawled the orders toward the rear and minced away. Zack had seen her kind in scores of prairie and desert towns, women alone in a rough man's world and forced to meet them on their own terms. Some managed to remain intact in hope of marriage, while others settled for transciency and numbers. He felt her eyes on him, sizing him up as she probably did every new man.

"Where's Ty?" Bernie asked eagerly.

"Sleeping one off."

"Here?" Bernie gasped. "In Piute?"

"Over in the Nevada Hotel."

"Well, think of that!" Bernie breathed. "Old Ty's back, too. Where've you boys been hiding out?"

"Nebraska, mostly," Zack said. "We went to Wyoming from here. You still up on the desert?"

"Same miserable old place. You probably don't know

7

my old man died two or three years ago. I'm running the outfit—such as it is."

Bernie's sorrow, Zack decided, stemmed more from the sorry condition of the Quick outfit than the loss of a father Bernie had never liked. Thurm Quick had been a rough man with no understanding of boys. Bernie had felt the end of a tug strap more than once, and in light of later understanding Zack wondered if this was what had drawn Bernie to the Maxons so strongly.

"Is Evalyn still up there?" Zack asked.

"Same old place. All she's got left is her mother, now. And no ranch. Sam Milliron bought part of it, Ed Larkin the rest. You wouldn't know Ed—he's new. Come down from the Powder a few years ago and bought the old Hawkeye. Evalyn runs a kind of roadhouse there at the old headquarters. Lots of travel through that country now, with the railroad down here. You boys haven't been up there?"

Zack shook his head. "Only got in on yesterday's train. I figure on going up today. Ty was going, too, but he won't feel like it."

"Wait till tomorrow and go with me."

"You and Ty are going to sleep," Zack said, "but I'm blamed if I care to hang around this place all day."

"She's a lot better at night," Bernie agreed.

Stella brought them coffee, then their breakfasts, and afterward lingered expectantly.

"This is Zack Maxon," Bernie said grudgingly. "He grew up around here."

"No fooling?" Stella said.

Zack only smiled at her, and her matching smile as she swayed away told him she was glad he had come back.

"Now, I've been trying to get on her good side for months," Bernie said in disgust. "You Maxons always did have it. Your old man was a ladykiller, according to my old man, and Evalyn never could see me for you and Ty."

"For Ty," Zack said reflectively. "She couldn't see either of us for him."

"He probably does more about things like that, now."

Zack gave him a quick frown, not liking that kind of insinuation when it came to Evalyn Trahan.

They moved on into reminiscence. From what Bernie

8

had to say about the Piute, while they ate their meal, it hadn't changed a great deal. Ben Newkirk still ran cattle on the north end of the Garnets. Jake Michaels was in the foothills west of the Quick outfit, while Loren Lee still wrung an uncertain living from his spread between the south end of the Garnets and that particular stretch of dry hell called the Smoke Tree Desert. Sam Milliron was where he had always been, cast against Red Cedar Mountain but enlarged since he had bought part of the old Trahan ranch.

"You wouldn't know Nancy," Bernie concluded.

"Who's she?"

"Don't you remember Nancy Milliron?"

"Oh, yeah—that button."

Bernie whistled. "No more. That scrawny colt turned into the prettiest little filly you ever seen, and nobody's put a halter on her yet."

Zack could remember the shy, gawky girl of around ten who had always seemed afraid of him because he was one of the wild Maxon boys. He listened amiably while Bernie rambled on, thinking that the old restlessness still drove this man, for when Bernie wasn't talking he was moving some part of his body or blinking his pale eyes in the way Zack remembered.

Finally, his face sobering, Bernie said, "You're going to throw a scare into 'em up there."

"Why should we?"

"They've all got guilty consciences."

"Nobody worried about acquiring one that night."

Bernie stared thoughtfully. "That's right, you wouldn't know. They caught that horse thief with the goods. After they'd killed your dad for it, trying to take and hang him."

Zack felt a hot, seering jolt between his shoulders; the shock of it climbed into his brain and exploded there. His first thought, afterward, was: God, I hope Ty doesn't find that out . . . Then he knew that it made little difference. Nothing could make Ty hate them any worse than he did already: Ben Newkirk, Jake Michaels, Loren Lee, Sam Milliron, four of the men who had surrounded the cabin on Red Cedar Mountain in the night but failed to take Kelsey Maxon alive.

There were three desert regions north of the railroad. The Smoke Tree and Red Rock were joined just north of Piute town by a narrow neck and were true wastelands. Beyond, the spring-fed Piute Desert, graced by waterholes, white sage and bunchgrass, was classified as waste by the land office because it received annually less than the twenty inches of rainfall considered essential to agrarian success. Zack was crossing the blistering neck between Smoke Tree and Red Rock on a horse obtained at the livery, an hour after having breakfast with Bernie Quick.

He was seeing the forecountry with new vision now that he had several years of real cattle experience behind him. He could discern the hazy, purple ends of the Garnets to the left, separated by hills from Red Cedar Mountain. Beyond that were the vegas, running east as far as the Red Rock extended and sweeping north to a prosperous, stream-fed range around Pinnacle Lake. Now, with so many years in the Nebraska sandhill and butte country, he knew that this was good cattle land except that it had been divided among too many small-time operators for any one of them to build much of a ranch.

He came off the hot narrows in less than an hour, his shirt sticking to his back, sweat standing wet on his neck and hands. He had forgotten how hot it could get here in July. The desert was a bleak, empty region that could destroy a man not onto its ways as surely—and more horribly—than a gun could do the job. Its creatures, plant and animal, in the fierce struggle to live had equipped themselves with tough fibres, thorns or claws, and learned to live through the extremes of season and in the eternal struggle of kind against kind. Even the men who came here underwent this adaptation; they had to or they went the way of all waste.

His gaze ran across the simmering flatness where as yet there was little save sandy earth, scorified rock and the toughest of desert plants and reptiles. But forward the brown low hills between the mountains flowed for some fifteen miles like the tawny, naked curves of a recumbent woman. There began the cattle country, sealed off by desert. There he had spent over half the years of his life. There had begun a thing that had influenced him each day since he left.

Five miles out of Piute he reached a forks where the

10

Alta trail veered for California from the old north road, and he kept straight forward. Afterward Red Cedar slipped along on his right, lying on the land like a half-plucked fowl because of its cedars. He looked with curiosity toward the Milliron headquarters as he rode by, and remembered that Sam Milliron had been a kindly enough fellow even though he had taken part in the night attack on the Maxon cabin. He remembered Bernie's mention of the now grown Nancy, the way his eyes had come alive with a hungry heat. It was surprising that she had become an attractive woman when all he could recall was a plain kid who had been afraid of him and thus had earned his own dislike.

The old Trahan headquarters had been right on the north road and, ten miles north of the Alta fork, he came to them. During the approach the place looked the same as ever although perhaps better kept, but when he rode in where the road widened he saw how the big old house under the trees had been converted into a wayside tavern. Now that cattle no longer were worked there, the old system of corrals, save for one, had disappeared from around the barn across the road. This was a depressing change to him. When a ranch died it was like a man's going, for the ranch and the man were one thing.

He swung down at the hitchrack that ran along the edge of the porch, and looked up at the sign that said: BAR, MEALS AND LODGINGS. The whole site showed upkeep; the house had received a coat of white over its mottled tan, and there was a larger window in front through which he could see into a barroom. Tying the horse, he gained the porch and went in.

Evelyn Trahan was seated on something behind the bar. She was concentrating on some work, apparently her accounts, and wrote something down before she looked up at him. She did not immediately recognize him, and he stood there a moment, his hand still on the knob of the door, looking across at her. He had remembered her as loveliness and it was no magnified memory for she was lovely still.

Her shiny dark hair still had its lazy natural curl, her face was still exquisite in its molding, and her eyes, as she glanced obliquely toward him, had that old pleasure-kindling power. But she had matured; the girl was now a

11

woman, and his stare apparently irritated her for she spoke coolly.

"Good morning."

Without speaking, he walked across to her and began to smile. Even as he said, "Hello, Evelyn," he saw her mind awaken to him, the eyes leaping with their old liveliness, the lips breaking into a matching smile.

"Why—it's Zack!"

Yet she did not move off the stool and come around to him. Instead she reached her arms across the bar, her hands clutching his and holding onto them, fiercely possessive.

She whispered, "You came back!"

"And Ty's in Piute."

"Ty, too? I can't believe it!"

"How about a drink on it, anyhow?" he asked.

She looked at him in sudden uneasiness, and he watched her face stiffen with some secret stoicism to wipe this out. Withdrawing her hands from his, she reached resolutely down and when she brought the hands up past the bar edge he saw that she held crutches. His breath knifed into his lungs, and he had trouble restraining the shock of it from his face.

She didn't look at him thereafter, only swinging from the stool to the support of the crutches, and he watched her slender shoulders shoot up in a hump as her weight settled. It wasn't the change in her appearance that appalled him, it was this knowledge for the first time received.

"Let's have it at the table," she said.

Shifting a distance behind the bar, she placed a bottle and glasses on the top. He picked them up blindly, unable to accept this thing. There was no need for her to come out from behind the bar, but he saw from the set of her eyes that she was resolved upon it. She thumped along to its end and as she came around a pain again sliced through him. There was no point in averting his eyes, he dared not do it. One of her legs touched the floor as she moved; the other hung limp and small and shortened. She stood before him as a woman might stand denuded for a man's inspection, it was that hard for her to do.

"Evalyn," he breathed, "I never dreamed it was that bad."

12

Then, because he had done no pretending, she eased and smiled at him. "It's all right, Zack, and it wasn't anybody's fault—but their's. You and Ty couldn't have done any more than you did. The wound wasn't bad, but there was a nerve involved, and that's what did it. But that drink! I want to hear all about you and Ty."

They had a drink on their reunion and afterward talked in alternating rushes. She had little to add to what Bernie had told him about the country. Her father had died not long after the trouble in which the Maxon boys had left the desert. The land had been sold, the money going to keep her and her mother until, matured, Evalyn had invested the rest in converting the house to a wayside tavern.

They did well. There was much freighting and passenger travel out of Piute, now that it was on a railroad, and the traffic for northeastern California and southeastern Oregon passed here. Her mother was not in good health, kept to herself most of the time upstairs, but Evalyn got along quite well with the help of a husband and wife team working for her. In turn Zack told her that he and Ty meant to go on to California when they had made a short visit. This disappointed her, but he wanted her to know that right away. The mere knowledge of Ty's return had enlivened her notably.

Neither of them mentioned what had happened on Red Cedar Mountain, so changing all their lives, and because he knew her work pressed he left shortly with a promise to return with Ty before they left for the coast. Then he rode out and when he reached the old turn-off to the mountain an overpowering impulse came to him and he knew he was going up there.

On this side Red Cedar climbed sharply; beyond its summit it flattened, then began a gentle fall toward the level, watered vegas that ran east. The road showed no travel yet each step of the horse aroused in him an old memory. The horse soon topped out and afterward followed a bare trace on through the thin trees. A half hour later he came to it: a shack whose roof had collapsed from the weight of snow long ago, and that was all that was left up here of his old life.

13

2

If Kelsey Maxon had a calling, it was that of horse trapper. The wild ones ran throughout the wastes, from Red Cedar to the Catlow plateau and thence east to the breaks of the Owyhee River. When he was pinched for money, Kelsey would take his two sons—and often young Bernie, although Thurm Quick did not like it—and make up a camp and head out. The trapping was high adventure: the matching of wits with a highly intelligent animal, the strategy that beat it, the thrilling runs that completed the capture. Afterward twenty or thirty of the best of the mustangs, mixed with gentled horses, would be trailed to Red Cedar, topped off and sold.

It was this devotion to horses and his long periods of idleness that made Kelsey a suspect when some more valuable animals vanished off a desert ranch. Nobody knew whether the whisperings of his guilt were true—they didn't have to be proved for a whisper carried its own cogency. There were times when even his sons didn't know where he was, and on more than one occasion such an absence had coincided with the loss of livestock. Without a mother, Kelsey's sons grew wild and made trouble in the harmless but irritating way of boys. So when the blow-up came it had involved the whole family.

At fifteen Zack had been overgrown, his legs too long for his trunk, his head too small. Physically, except for his tallness, he resembled his mother, Kelsey said. His nature, other than for Kelsey's untamed disposition, came from her also. Ty, on the other hand, duplicated his father from pubescence on, possessing the same lithe, tapered body, the dark coloring.

With Bernie Quick they formed a neighborhood gang of which Evalyn Trahan was a sometime member because she lived near them and there were no girls her

14

age on the desert. They had no conscious grievance against the others, and mostly they hunted, trapped or rode or loafed together, taking their time about growing up. It was probably because of Kelsey that they got such a bad name.

Kelsey had done a lot of things in his time: a little mining around the Comstock and down in the Esmeralda, a lot more cow punching along the Humboldt, and once he had driven a freight outfit out of Reno. But always he had been drawn to the wilderness, the only place where he felt alive and free, and for that reason had been attracted to the Indians.

At the time of his death he was still in his early forties. The sap of life had always been high in him, the yearning for a woman's companionship and favors too strong to be denied completely. When this need would rise in him, nagging until he acted, he had for years slipped away to the reservation where he had many friends, and there he would arrange for some young woman to go with him into the mountains for a while. Afterward he would reward her with presents and return home. He hoped his sons were too young to figure out where he had been.

The culmination of this satisfying if suspect life had been abrupt, although Kelsey must have known it would come. It was hardest on Ty, who was his father's obvious favorite and who felt something close to hero worship for the strangely lonely man. Ty had been happy that night when Kelsey rode in after an absence. The sons had spent the day by themselves, and it was good to have him home.

After supper, his pipe going, Kelsey sat at the table and for the first time talked about the future to his sons. As he listened, Zack had a feeling that something worried his father, something that had happened while he was away.

"You boys have trapped a lot of mustangs," Kelsey commented. "You know what happens when they let a spook turn them a different way to what they want to go. Pretty soon another spook turns them again, till finally they're in a trap they can't get out of." He laughed. "That's how it goes with a man, sometimes. He's turned and turned until he's caught. I never could stand

15

the thought of that. I never wanted it for you boys. But I was wrong. That's not right for you boys."

"Nothing's happened, has it?" Zack said in a tight voice.

"It's apt to," Kelsey admitted, his face darkening. "And if it does it's a trap I got into because I took too many wrong turns. There's different ways a man can get scared. Some don't mind danger, I never did. But they spook off from other things and end in a trap just the same."

Worriedly, Zack said, "What's going to happen, Kelsey?"

Kelsey never answered that question. At that moment a horse ran into the dark yard—it must have been ten o'clock by then—and moving quickly to the door Zack saw Evalyn slide off her pony and come racing toward him.

"Where's Kelsey?" she cried as she brushed past Zack. She stared with wide eyes at the man still at the table. "You've got to get out of here, Kelsey! They're coming to get you! They—they're going to hang you!"

Kelsey sprang out of his chair. "Who is, Evalyn?" he asked her.

"Nearly everybody! My father heard them planning. But he doesn't want a hand in it, and neither does Thurm Quick. He was afraid to tip you off, but I slipped out my window. There can't be much time left, Kelsey— you've got to go!"

"You're imagining things," Kelsey said, but Zack doubted that he meant it. "Maybe he heard them say I ought to be hung. I've been told that to my face."

"No, sir!" Evalyn insisted. At thirteen a womanliness was coming to her that showed in her tense body. "Jake Michaels had some horses stolen—six of them. They were driven north and today Ben Newkirk saw you coming from that direction."

"I thought he did," Kelsey said, his face falling. "You get on home, Evalyn. Right now."

"Not unless you all leave here."

"You boys to along with her," Kelsey ordered.

"Not me," Ty said promptly, and Zack shook his head.

They had no choice, anyway, for Evalyn had waited long for her opportunity to slip away from the ranch with a warning. Even as the sons stared stubbornly at their

16

father a shot crashed out, a bullet cut through the door, then a voice rang loudly.

"Maxon! Get your hands up and come out of there!"

The shot was to show they meant business, and Zack thought the voice belonged to Sam Milliron, who also had lost horses that summer. They had seen Evalyn's pony and realized they had lost their chance for surprise. Kelsey stood frozen through a long breath, then stepped forward and blew out the lamp. Zack winced at the unfairness of it. They knew Kelsey couldn't put up a fight with Evalyn and his sons caught with him in the shack. They were taking advantage of that.

Raising his voice, Kelsey yelled, "I'm not coming, Sam, but you let these kids get out!"

"You come with them, Maxon!" Milliron replied.

A second bullet cut through the boards of the wall, another warning or possibly a jumpy shot. Evalyn let out a small cry, and in the obscurity Zack saw her fall to the floor. With the sound of an enraged animal, Kelsey sprang to where his rifle leaned against the wall. He seized it, knocked out a window pane and fired back. Immediately the siege was on.

"Down beside her, boys," Kelsey said between shots.

Zack crawled to where Evalyn lay quietly. "You all right?" he asked, afraid she wouldn't be able to answer him.

But she did, very weakly, "My hip."

He put his hand there, and her dress was wet. He called, "She wasn't just scared, Kelsey. She's hurt."

With a groan, Kelsey said, "I've got to give up."

"No!" Evalyn cried. "They'll hang you! I'm all right —it's hardly a scratch!"

Ty got his father's pistol and ran to another window. He knocked out the glass and began shooting into the night. Zack, lying beside Evalyn, wished he could believe her about not being hurt very bad. He could not believe it. By then her dress was mushy wet.

He whispered, "I've got to try and stop the bleeding, Evalyn."

"Go ahead."

The hole when he found it was at the top of her hip, toward the back. The bullet hadn't gone deep or it would have torn her open, and he wondered if it had lodged

17

against her spine. He knew how to apply a compress bandage to stop bleeding for Ty had once cut his foot badly with an axe while they were alone. Moving about, the sound of the firing jarring his ears, the powder exhaust in the room stinging his nose and eyes, he found his father's white shirt and tore it up. He got a compress on the bullet hole and more cloth wrapped around her body. She made no sound, and he realized she had passed out.

He moved her over against the windowless back wall. He barricaded her on the exposed sides with everything he could drag across the floor. Maybe it was then that he first knew how much he loved her.

After the first spasm of shooting, the thing quieted down, the men outdoors realizing that Kelsey meant business the same as they did. But the desert ranchers could afford to be patient, the windows and one door were the only way out of the shack. There were no more weapons, and Zack lay there beside Evalyn, listening to her light breath.

He was always to wonder why, in this violent hour, he had no fear for himself or Kelsey or Ty—only for Evalyn. As the firing died down he only wanted them to give it up and go away so he could get help for her. Yet it went on forever, each shot jarring him with an almost physical impact.

Then she opened her eyes, moved her head, and he whispered, "You all right again?"

"Yes. It doesn't feel like it's bleeding, anymore. And it doesn't hurt. I don't know what knocked me down."

"It come through the boards but had enough kick to do that. You'll be all right."

"But your father—he can't get away. And what's going to become of you and Ty?"

"Never mind about us."

"My father isn't out there, Zack," she whispered.

"I know. He never liked us much, but he's white."

"Kelsey didn't steal those horses, did he?"

"Of course he didn't," Zack returned, but in his mind he was no longer sure.

Presently the shooting stopped entirely, but Kelsey said quietly, "They're still out there, waiting for daylight. That's what I hoped they'd do. Boys, you listen now. They've

18

got me. I hadn't anything to do with them horses, but they won't give me a trial or they'd have had the sheriff come and get me. Before it gets light, you're going to get Evalyn and yourselves out of here."

"Not much," Ty said bitterly. "Anyhow, how could we?"

"I've always been afraid of something like this. I've had the name, and maybe sometimes I've had the game. There's some boards on the back wall that can be knocked off, and they're not covering that side. You can get from there to the brush at the spring, and after that it'll be easy. You're going, Ty. I won't have it any other way. You hear?"

Ty didn't answer.

Kelsey said they would wait as long as possible to try to throw the other side off guard. He would say when. And they waited through what to Zack were agonizing hours. He knew Kelsey's mind was made up, that this was the final trap and one which he would not try to escape. Zack would have agreed with Ty except for his fear for Evalyn. She had shown great courage to help them, had got hurt, and they owed her everything. Maybe it was disloyal, but his mind set on that alone, and he couldn't make it do anything else.

Finally Kelsey, with a surprisingly easy push, knocked off three of the upright boards on the back wall, proving he had fixed them, perhaps long ago, for just this purpose. He waited through a moment to see if the slight sound had attracted attention. Apparently it had not.

Quietly, he said, "Get going. Make it to the spring, then on into the cedars. If there's any way you can get some of their horses, take 'em. Get Evalyn home, but you boys keep going. They'd make you county wards, and God knows what would happen to you. You're old enough to take care of yourselves, now. At least I've taught you how to do that."

"I'm not going, Kelsey," Ty said.

"Boy, I want you to. That's all there is left that I do want. Just to see the three of you go."

Ty turned then, leaving the pistol because his father might need it. It was a rough, brutal thing they had to do after that, deserting Kelsey while knowing he would soon die, crawling across the open and dragging Evalyn be-

19

tween them until they could squirm into the brush by the spring. Kelsey had begun shooting again, and Zack knew it was to help them escape. The men ringing the house on the three other sides retaliated.

Crawling to the far side of the brush, Zack saw the horses, and that was how they got away. The thing he remembered most vividly afterward was that the morning star had hung over them, the signal of the return of light and life.

3

It grew too hot in this hotel room on the south side of the Nevada Hotel for anything but a desert lizard to sleep. Ty Maxon finally got his sticky eyelids to stay open and he lay with his glazed stare fixed on a curiously shaped blotch left by leaking rain on the faded paper of the ceiling. Its outlines put him in mind of a naked man humped under a great burden. He wondered what made up the load, why the fellow thought he had to carry it when he had only to toss it aside and straighten that poor back.

His nostrils felt like hot wires had been run into his head, his staring at the water mark had blurred his vision, but that was all that remained of what had been a large evening, his first in old Piute. He was not as powerfully built as Zack, being shorter and lighter, but he was as tough in physique. Drinking never knocked him out the way it did some men.

He wondered lazily where Zack had gone and didn't much care. He wasn't in Zack's rush to get on to California; he liked to take things easy. The only time recently he had been in a hurry, he thought pleasantly, was to get away from the prairies. Maybe he should have explained more about that since the boy—Ty always thought of his brother as being juvenile since he was the younger— since the boy had given up a good job to come with him.

20

He and Zack were as close as they had ever been but for several years now Ty had followed his father's practice of sudden, unexplained disappearances, the only difference being that he would be gone for months, always returning to Zack and being with him for even longer periods. He always explained where he had been although it was not often the truth. On the last venture things had gone a little wrong, and it had seemed expedient to make a change in surroundings, since a change in habits was less attractive to Ty.

When he swung off the bed finally it was with the same swift, lithe motion with which he did everything; and when he rose to his full, tapered height he yawned, feeling almost as good as he ever did when he first got up. He knew he was the image of Kelsey—people around here might consider him a haunt—with one important difference. He wasn't afraid of anything physical, mental or moral, as Kelsey had admitted being on the last day of his life.

Ty could remember his mother faintly, and he knew Zack was more like her except that he had Kelsey's vitality and temper. Part of Ty's impression of Carrie Maxon came from what his father had said. She had been sensible and steady, an altogether good woman who deserved a steady, sensible and altogether good husband instead of a wildling like Kelsey. They had met and married in Gold Hill, had lived there and in Reno and Pioche and Elko, being blessed, as it was fashionable to say, with two offspring and cursed by poverty and Kelsey's restless feet. Maybe Carrie had wanted to die after giving birth to Zack, and maybe Kelsey had wanted her to do it so he wouldn't have to keep making her unhappy. Ty often wondered about them, now that he knew something about men and women himself.

As he moved down through the hotel lobby, Ty noticed that it was after three o'clock. The dining room was closed until supper time. Stepping onto the street, he tried to recall the restaurant where Zack had taken him for coffee the night before; he remembered it as a pleasant place. A sign up the street said: ACME EATS, and as he came up to its front he saw it was the place and that it wasn't pleasant at all when he was sober.

The man who came from the rear to wait on him

21

wore a white shirt with dirty cuffs, and there was a fleck of dried egg on his flowing mustache. That lessened Ty's appetite, but he ordered coffee and a sandwich, which would do him until he connected with Zack again and they had a good supper at the hotel.

When he had brought the order the man said, "New here, ain't you?"

That was pretty obvious and certainly no oddity in a rail-head like Piute, but it was conversation. Ty decided to upset him, for the fellow was a little condescending, probably felt like a pioneer.

"As a matter of fact," Ty said, "I remember this place when there wasn't a railroad within fifty miles, let alone an Acme Eats."

"That a fact?" the man said with widening eyes. The derby, sack suit and diamond stickpin had him confused. "Raised around here?"

Ty laughed. "I guess you could say I was raised."

When he came back to the street he decided again that he liked the new town better than the old, not that it would stay this interesting when the construction work on through California was finished. Most of the new places were saloons offering gambling as well. One—the Big Chief—was a gambling hall also offering volatile spirits. A big circus-like tent housed the noisy Eden Dance Palace— some of the girls there were good looking—and on past that was a discreet, well patronized structure that was obviously the local bawdy house. The town looked deserted now but by dark the quiet would be banished.

He wouldn't mind staying around a while although Zack was anxious to get to California where they meant to pool their capital—maybe Zack wanted it done before it was blown—in a little ranch. That had been the agreement, the only terms on which Zack would quit the Union Cattle Company, where he had risen to a range boss's job.

Entering a saloon that called itself the Oasis—where in the dry country was there a town that didn't have one?—he took the day's first drink. Afterward he bought a handful of cigars, lighting one and stowing the rest in his vest. The aromatic taste of the smoke combined with the drink and light meal to restore him completely, ready for a new night of it.

22

He decided to check at the Elephant Livery to see if Zack had hired a horse, but as he came onto the sidewalk he saw a man he recognized instantly—Bernie Quick.

"I've been looking for you, you hyena!" Bernie yelled. "I was just up to your room! Ty, how are you?"

"Fat and sassy, Bernie," Ty said as they grabbed hands.

"Saw Zack this morning," Bernie said. "Told me you were sleeping one off, so I hit the hay myself. He said you weren't back to stay, man. Why not? Everything was forgotten a long time ago."

"Oh, was it?" Ty asked softly.

Bernie glanced at him shrewdly. "On this end."

"How about our end?

Thoughtfully, Bernie said, "No, I guess not. I wouldn't, in your place. Let's have a drink."

Bernie was in no hurry to go home to the Piute Desert; he got a bottle and glasses and took them to a back table, where they sat down. He accepted the cigar Ty offered and lighted it, smiling amiably.

Finally, he said, "Ty, I've wished a lot since my old man died that you were here. There's opportunity for a team like us."

Ty's eyes kindled with interest although he didn't want to feel that. Zack wanted to go on in two or three days, so why get excited about anything here, although privately he had been excited about coming, had stayed so ever since they arrived. But if Zack wanted to go on, they would.

There's one thing I'd like to know first, he thought. Who fired the shot that killed Kelsey? If I could do something about that, I'd never want to come back here again.

As if worried by something he saw on Ty's face, Bernie said, "My old man didn't have anything to do with it."

"I know. Evalyn was there. She said who was coming."

"That's right," Bernie said, nodding. "Poor kid."

"Why poor kid?"

"She's been on crutches ever since."

Ty's eyes widened as he remembered in a vivid rush how he and Zack had got her home and left immediately because Kelsey had ordered them to do it. Her wound hadn't seemed bad; she had insisted that it was trivial.

23

But maybe she had known, had gone through all that because she understood and had to help them. A sudden great tenderness rose in him. He hadn't remembered her in ages, but all at once he wanted to see her with a poignant longing.

"What I thought," Bernie was saying, "was that when Zack gets in we can make a night of it, then you boys come up to the ranch for a few days. No reason why you can't, is there?"

Probably there wasn't, Ty thought, as long as they got out of this town where money went like water, where a man could get into serious trouble at the drop of a hat.

Again doing some face reading, Bernie said comfortably, "We'll talk Zack into it."

They spent a couple of hours there while Bernie filled Ty in on things. It would be a lot of fun seeing what happened once word got around the desert that the Maxon boys were back—those hellions who now would bear a grudge as well. Bernie wanted the excitement of it, Ty began to want it hungrily for a very different reason. A part of him had died with Kelsey, a big part. Maybe he could resurrect if it he could balance the books better than they had been left that awful night.

Zack found them there around six. He looked relaxed, like he had enjoyed himself, and he seemed to take it for granted that Ty and Bernie would be half drunk. He had a drink himself, then they went to supper in the hotel dining room. Ty ate with relish, the first substantial food he had had all day, and Bernie matched him bite for bite. It made Ty think of their campfires and more poignantly of the meals Kelsey would cook for them, for he was an expert at it.

All at once he said fiercely, "Who killed Kelsey, Bernie?"

"I don't know. They know, but not a one would ever talk about it. But they're all guilty, and they've acted like it ever since the real horse thief was caught."

"How's that?" Ty's words sounded like two shots.

Bernie stared up at him. "I guess it was Zack I told. They got the man with Michaels' horses, and he cleared Kelsey. That was only a few days after it happened."

"God damn them," Ty said bitterly.

Bernie nodded.

24

Zack was scowling. He didn't like this run of talk, but Ty no longer cared whether he did or didn't. He had never believed his father guilty, Kelsey had claimed to the last that he wasn't, yet having it proved lent the thing a cogency that moved him powerfully. They couldn't wait, they couldn't let the law handle it. They had to try to take Kelsey out and hang him. The injustice of that greatly sharpened the grief that had never died in him.

As if prodding that wound deliberately, Bernie said, "You know what Jake Michaels said when they found out, and him in on it? That it was good riddance, anyhow."

Ty felt as though his head would explode; even Zack looked bitterly angry. Zack had cared for Kelsey but never in the worshipful way Ty had.

Afterward Bernie went down to the livery to see how they were treating his horse. He had always loved animals, even stray dogs and cats and hurt wildlings and at the same time could try to gouge out somebody's eyes in a fight. When it came to people there were few he really liked, and Ty understood how that was—at least you could learn an animal's ways and depend on it to stay in character.

Up in the room with Zack, Ty said, "How about it, kid? Do we spend a few days with Bernie?"

Zack shook his head doubtfully.

"Why not?"

"He isn't good for us. It struck me that he hates them worse than you do."

"That's impossible. He's the same old Bernie."

"Yeah. But are we the same?"

Emphatically, Ty said, "I am."

Zack turned back from the window, his face stern. "Well, maybe I'm not. Trying to even old scores wouldn't get us a thing but trouble, and I've had enough. If we're going to have our own ranch, let's have it. Let's raise some steers and horses. Maybe sometime I'd like to get married."

"Married?" Ty said. "Why buy a horse when you can ride another man's?"

Zack turned again to the window, and Ty stared at the back of his head. Irritation was as natural to himself as breathing, but Zack rarely showed it, going along

25

amiably unless something happened to light his fuse. Then Ty remembered something and mentioned it.

"See Evalyn up there?"

"Yeah."

"Bernie told me about her. Was she fooling us that night?"

"She was. And she wants to see you."

"I want to see her, too. Let's stay with Bernie a couple of days, anyhow."

"All right," Zack agreed. "But I'm warning you. He's trying to rope us into something, at least you. He's got something on his mind."

Ty had the same feeling about Bernie Quick, but his attitude toward it was different. There were old scores to settle and this had been much on his mind for years. He and Bernie had been good running mates and could be again. He wanted to stay indefinitely, at least until he had gained some degree of satisfaction here. But he didn't want to part with Zack yet, even on amiable terms.

He knew that he had many times been unfair to Zack who, with his mother's stability, wanted steadiness in his life. He remembered how they had gone to the Crooked River from here and worked for an outfit for nearly a year. Zack had liked it, but the next summer a driver had wanted a crew to take a herd to eastern Wyoming. Ty had been eager to go, so Zack agreed.

They had drifted to Texas, later, and come back to North Platte with another herd, and had ridden for the big Union Cattle Company that had ranches all through that part of the country. Zack had worked up, but the next spring Ty made a trip by himself into western Montana. He could always get on with Union himself, since he was a tophand. Now he had drawn Zack away from them, and he felt the responsibility of that.

Dismissing that because it depressed him, he said, "Well, let's see if Bernie can show us anything about this town we didn't discover last night."

Zack was exploring his face in a strange, disturbed way, wondering about too many things. His penetrating gaze seemed to cut into his brother, making Ty aware of a feeling of guilt, of regret that their differences in nature and in character might turn out to be more potent than the shared things that had always held them together.

26

"You go on," Zack said finally. "I don't feel like another night of it."

At the door Ty looked back, a dry smile tightening the ends of his mouth. He said, "Don't worry, kid." Zack's face did not change, and Ty stepped through the doorway. Shutting the door gave him the feeling he always gained when he had left his brother to go on his own: a sense of freedom, of transition into another world that Zack could never enter and share. The regrets and uncertainties had begun to fade even while he crossed the lobby.

On the street he pulled in a long, satisfied breath, the night before him and Bernie to share it. It struck him that Bernie was like another brother to him, each playing his role, filling a need. The night's strident voice was lifting over the town. He heard a piano's tinny merriment somewhere along the street. A puncher coming around the corner of the farther end let out a raucous yell and ran his horse forward, drilling up a thick dust.

This was the pulsating new vitality of Piute town, and north on the desert was an old thing: the men who had killed Kelsey Maxon.

4

Ever since the railroad had drawn riffraff to the country, Nancy Milliron had avoided meeting strangers on the road or range. She was especially careful up here on Red Cedar where she often came when she felt restless and lonely, although it was odd that she would seek a yet greater loneliness and be able to find comfort in it. Because it paid to watch out these days, she halted on the ridge when she saw down below at the old Maxon cabin a man standing with a bowed head, staring at the ruins through an interminable period.

Then, because she had never been short on curiosity, she turned the horse along the ridge through the cedars. When again she reined in, she could see him better. She

27

was at once struck by a feeling of familiarity, yet she watched the motionless, preoccupied fellow through several moments before she began to wonder if he was one of the Maxons. No one else would be interested in anything except firewood in that old ruins.

Things buried in her mind rose to the surface and moved her strongly. Nobody knew better than she her father's regret of his actions up here that night when he, like the others, had let passion overcome judgment. She remembered what it had been like when they learned that Kelsey Maxon had had nothing to do with the stolen Michaels horses, perhaps not even with those her father had lost earlier that summer. This guilt had troubled her too, mixed however, with the equally strong childhood memory of the hell-raising Maxon boys.

In her motionless spying she could hear the wind streaming over Red Cedar as it crossed the desert. Its motion through the trees struck up a low sibilance and its pressure billowed the foliage and bent the cedars' tips like heads all nodding to the west. The odor of summer was on the wind, the smell of dryness and heat and of nameless things out of the desert's mysterious deep. Above the mountain the same currents pushed row after row of light-struck clouds across the ridge into a lost sky.

When the man at the cabin finally mounted and rode nearer the feeling of familiarity grew more pronounced. When he passed below her and she saw that his hair was red, she knew it was the younger brother—Zack—the one she had feared less because, for all his reputation, there was something gentle in his manner.

She waited where she was long enough to let him get well ahead, then followed, no longer wanting to be up there, deciding that what she needed was company, that she would go up to see Evalyn and Mamma Trahan. Evalyn was not often busy this time of day, but if she happened to be Mamma always liked company. She was a lost, unhappy woman, too lazy, in Nancy's opinion, to do anything to improve her lot. Sam Milliron said his daughter was hard to fool, and Nancy hoped that this was true; it was very easy to go wrong in a country as treacherous as the desert.

Seeing Zack Maxon made her remember what a child she had been when the brothers left the Piute. She was

28

glad she had become an attractive woman when for so long that had been in doubt. Yet it had done her little good to this point, for the only young, unattached men on the desert were Ed Larkin and Bernie Quick. Ed was hopelessly in love with Evalyn, had been ever since he came to the desert, while something in Bernie's hot, prying eyes would make the flesh of anyone but a dance hall girl contract and creep. She had had trouble with Bernie more than once. She wondered if both Maxon boys were back, if they were going to stay and, if so, whether they would take up again with Bernie. If they did it would prove that they were as bad as when they went away.

Nancy reached the north road and turned right. The heat came fully on her at that lower level, but she was used to the extremes of winter and summer and never noticed. She rode with a complete, unconscious skill, a slender girl with long legs accustomed to the saddle. Her hair was almost light enough to be called blond but not quite, and she wore it in braids about her head. Her arms were slender but not bony, and her shoulders widened just enough to match the long arch of her thighs. She had yet to learn that none of these graces equaled in charm the fresh zest for living that was so rare in the Piute.

Evalyn was working on her books when Nancy came into the tavern. She looked up and smiled.

"Hello, Nancy. I was wondering when you were going to come up to see me. What have you been doing?"

"What a question," Nancy said. "What am I ever doing but killing time?"

"Seems to me you work hard enough."

"I didn't mean work."

"I know," Evalyn said thoughtfully. "And there isn't much else on the desert, is there? Anyhow, for a woman."

Nancy climbed onto the stool across the bar from Evelyn, thinking that over. There was certainly no lack of work, a woman could be at that from daylight to dark if she let it dominate her. There just wasn't much of what a woman really wanted to be had, and she found herself wondering again why so many who came here had died young. Her mother had, so had the Maxon boys', and she hadn't even been exposed to the Piute. Loren Lee and Jake Michaels had reached middle age without finding women willing to share their lives. Besides herself and

Evalyn, only Ben Newkirk's wife and Mamma Trahan had lived here very long. Mamma's spirit seemed to have been broken a long time ago, while Daycie Newkirk was little more than the bitchy, half-witted wife of a dried out old man.

Not liking that run of thought, Nancy said, "Who do you suppose I saw on Red Cedar a while ago?"

Evalyn frowned slightly. "So he went up there. I hoped he wouldn't, that he wanted to forget all that."

"You've seen him?"

"He was here. They're both back." Evalyn's color rose a little; she seemed happy and yet disturbed. "I guess it's natural Zack would want to see the old place. They lived there a long while."

"I wouldn't want to, after what you three went through."

"I've never gone back again." Evalyn's laugh was a little harsh. "One reason being the road's got so bad you can't drive a buggy up there."

Nancy wished she hadn't brought the subject up, knowing how much Evalyn had once liked to ride a horse. She said, "Is Mamma upstairs?"

"Go up and see her. She's feeling neglected."

As she climbed the stairs to the second floor, Nancy reflected that Mamma's feeling of neglect was nothing unusual. Everyone called the big, doll-faced woman that, as Evalyn did, because there was about her a look of maternal capacity where there was no such capacity at all. Mamma had to be babied all the time. She was a heavy woman with huge ankles, with a walk so slow and ponderous she disliked even to stand.

When Nancy stepped into the upstairs room, Mamma was in her heavy rocking chair, which Tom Trahan had built especially for her and laced with heavy strips of rawhide—and she rocked the chair as if in unison with her audible breath. The chair was by the window where she could watch the road, which she did constantly from morning to night. She was double-chinned and wore her white hair in a high pompadour so that her wide straight sides seemed only to step back somewhat to form a wide, straight neck and head.

Something had disturbed the heavy, square face of the woman, and Nancy knew at once what it was. Mamma

30

had seen Zack Maxon come here and she hated him, holding both the boys responsible for what had happened to to Evalyn, rather than the man who had actually shot and crippled her.

Wishing she hadn't come here at all, Nancy said, "Hello, Mamma. I can't stay, but maybe I'll go to town tomorrow. Is there anything I can get you?"

"I guess not. Ed Larkin was in the other day, and he's so good about things like that." The big woman stared intently at Nancy. "You'd better warn you father that Zack Maxon's back. He was here this morning."

"They're both back," Nancy said. She felt something tighten in her breast for she had not wondered until that moment if they had come back for revenge.

"As if they hadn't made trouble enough," Mamma said bitterly. "Evalyn's mooned over that Ty ever since they went away, and Ed worshiping the ground she walks on. I never wanted her to run with that pack, but her father said she needed company and they were the best to be had. But look what it done to her—ruined her whole life!"

Nancy wanted to tell Mamma Trahan that she had done little to improve that life, that Evalyn had probably gotten more from the Maxon boys and even Bernie Quick than she had ever received from her own mother. Sam Milliron had spoken often about this woman's neglect of her husband and child, of the complete self-centeredness of her restricted little world. Mamma's regret even now came less from Evalyn's tragedy than from her refusal to marry Ed Larkin, who was especially good to Mamma.

"There's no reason to suppose they're here to make trouble because of what happened that night," Nancy said. She turned, wanting to leave.

"Your father and the others better not depend on that, Nancy."

"I'll tell him," Nancy said. "Goodbye."

Mamma didn't answer for someone else was arriving, apparently. The woman peered out the window intently, her eyelids lifting widely as she slanted her gaze down to the road in front of the tavern. Nancy moved toward the stairs and descended.

The front half of the lower floor was now divided be-

31

tween a dining room and bar, a wide arch joining them into one large and pleasant space. As she reached the bottom of the stairs coming down the partial wall, Nancy saw that the arrivals were ranchers from across the range —old Newkirk with Michaels and Lee. They were shabby, dusty, unshaved men and, looking at Evalyn, Nancy saw a sudden cold satisfaction in her eyes. These were the other men who had been on Red Cedar, that night.

As they came through the doorway they were laughing about something that might have been off-color for they sobered when they saw the two women. Then they called greetings and walked across to the bar, their pant legs curving so they all looked bow-legged, spurs jingling as their heels hit the floor. Nancy waited at the foot of the stairs, not wanting to leave without another word with Evalyn. She hoped Evalyn would tap the bell on the end of the bar to call Lafe Peebles.

Evalyn's help came and went. At present a married couple from Piute worked here, the woman running the kitchen and helping with the rooms that were rented out. Her husband was the outside man, but he also waited on table and relieved Evalyn occasionally in the bar. Yet Evalyn swung off the stool onto her crutches. Nancy used her hand to motion a goodbye, but Evalyn called, "Don't go yet, Nancy."

Although this was a respectable place, it made Nancy feel awkward to be in the bar while men were drinking. Evalyn slung down in front of the men and set up the house bottle and glasses.

"What are you doing over here this time of day?" she asked.

"Been up to Pinnacle Lake," Loren Lee answered, "and it was only a little out of the way to come by and wet our whistles. And learn what's new. What is, Evalyn?" She was a clearing house for information, not because she was a busybody but because the Piute men gathered here more often than anywhere else.

The dislike that everyone bore Lee may have been the only thing causing the strange expression on Evalyn's face, but Nancy wondered. Evalyn watched them pour their drinks, then said in a casual way, "Not much except that the Maxon boys are back. Zack was here this morning."

Jake Michaels' hand came up and rubbed across his

mouth. He swung his head to stare at Ben Newkirk, who in turn had his eyes fixed unmovingly on Evalyn. Loren Lee's small body seemed to twitch. Nancy suddenly wondered whether Evalyn wanted the Maxons to punish these men for what they had done to her as well as to their father. One of Sam Milliron's regrets was that they had not let the youngsters come out of that cabin as Kelsey Maxon had asked. But someone had thrown a hasty shot, starting the fight, and that had settled it.

"I'll be go to hell," Ben Newkirk said finally. "Well, I always expected it, and there'll be the devil to pay, now." His aging face had a slack, almost resigned expression. For twenty-odd years the desert had confronted him with more than his limited powers could handle. His long-shafted body slumped into a more pronounced stoop, and Nancy wondered if he was remembering his part in that long ago affair as the man who had pointed the finger of guilt at Kelsey Maxon.

Michaels, burly and rough, was always the one quick with bluster. In a rash, rankled voice, he said, "Well, it was an honest mistake, and if they're looking for trouble they can have it. We run 'em out once, and if they ask for it, we can do it again."

"They've grown up since then, Jake," Evalyn said tartly.

Michaels flung her a quick, annoyed glance, then tossed off his drink. Loren Lee's wispy body kept moving restlessly, he was frightened and unable to hide it. Then, when old Newkirk downed his whisky, Lee did likewise and shuddered. They paid up and went out.

Coming forward, Nancy said, "I don't blame you for hating them and my father and even me. Evalyn, do you want them to take revenge?"

Evalyn looked at her musingly. "Honey, I don't hate you. Nor your father. He was the only one of them that was man enough to admit his mistake and show remorse. I see pain in his eyes every time he looks at me and remembers. But the others—! It's common gossip that Jake Michaels is carrying on an affair with old Newkirk's wife. Yet when the truth came out about Kelsey Maxon, Jake said it was good riddance of bad rubbish, anyway. Loren Lee is as dirty a little coward as ever lived, and a failure in every other respect. But it's not revenge I want. I want to see Ty

33

and Zack prove to them how wrong they were, how shoddy this bunch is. I want—well, never mind."

"I think I know what else you want. And I hope you get it, Evalyn."

5

The two days they were to spend on Bernie Quick's ranch stretched into three, then four. Although Bernie had disparaged it, Zack found to his surprise that Bernie's low estimate of his layout was not accurate. It was still a one-man outfit, with only four or five hundred steers lost in the brown hills and wearing the old T-Q. Bernie had done little to improve the spread over what it had been in Thurm Quick's day, but he had plans, and the possibilities wer there.

Bernie showed them around, not saying much but plainly thinking about something. Although they had covered the same ground many times as boys, Zack now saw it with experienced eyes. The range would carry twice the cattle Bernie ran, as he claimed, but that wasn't all. Bernie explained the rest one evening while they sat under the old tree by the house, the stars brilliantly shining above them.

"Loren Lee could be talked into selling out," he stated. "If a man had his spread and this he could run cattle from Milliron's to the Garnets and have the summer grass in the mountains, as well. What's two sorry ranches would make one good one, holding everything north of the Smoke Tree to Jake Michaels'."

"Why don't you buy Lee out?" Zack asked.

Bernie laughed. "For one thing, he would want to be paid for it. But why don't you and Ty? Land comes high in California these days, and there's hardly any open range. The fence problem's bad, now there's so many farms and orchards. They raise a little beef yet, but it sure ain't cow country anymore. This is and always will be because it's no good for anything else."

34

Zack was interested, but he had questions. "If Lee's been lucky to make a living off his spread, how would two of us make out?"

"Loren's no cowman," Bernie said readily. "Another thing, I've been talking about one good ranch. Why don't we throw in together? I'll put up T-Q against the money you figured to spend on the other side of the Sierra."

"He's got an idea there, Zack," Ty said. He sounded deeply interested.

Zack tossed away his cigarette, cautious suddenly. The thought of a partnership with Bernie had not come into his own mind until now, and it seemed to be the part Ty liked best. How wise would that be, and in the midst of old enemies, as well? Supposing he agreed—would Bernie and Ty be satisfied to remain hemmed against the Smoke Tree desert by those same enemies? Yet it would make a good cattle setup, better than they could hope for across the mountain—and there was Evalyn Trahan.

They had been over to her place every evening until this one, when Bernie had wanted to talk business. The moment he saw her look at Ty, Zack had known that it lay with her as it always had. Ty had seemed interested in her, in return, and she might be what he needed. Finally, so far Ty had made no effort to contact the men he so bitterly hated nor even mentioned them, although they had planned until now to leave on the day following.

"Where'd we get more cattle?" Ty was musing. "Over in California?"

Bernie made a disgusted sound. "We'd bring in Shorthorns from Oregon or Idaho. They're better rustlers, hardier, and easier to range. We'd weed out that scrub stock of Loren's as fast as we could, get us a few blooded bulls." He laughed. "Hit hard times, and we could hunt horses again for extra money. Still plenty up in the Owyhee. I haven't been there since the last time I went with you and Kelsey. I'd like to pack out on a trip like that right now. Damn it, boys, I wish you'd do it."

"I never found another place," Ty reflected, "that I liked as well as Red Cedar and the Piute. There's everything here, anything a man could want. Kid, how about it?"

"I just don't know," Zack confessed.

"If you still want California, then California it is."

"Somebody's coming," Bernie said, springing up.

35

They listened to the drumming of a horse drift across the night. It grew louder, from the southwest. For a long way in that direction there was nothing but empty country, which made this approach unusual. A horse and rider emerged in the starlight, coming toward T-Q headquarters.

"It's Ed Larkin," Bernie decided. "Must have been down to Susanville. He's got a married sister there."

As the horseman pulled up, Zack saw a tall, thin man in the saddle. "Howdy, Ed," Bernie greeted him. "Been down to Susietown? Light down and meet some old friends."

Standing after he had swung out of the saddle, Ed Larkin looked almost skinny. He pushed his peaked hat to the back of his head, and Zack saw that his lean face was young, strong. He said, "Howdy," twice as he shook hands with Zack, then Ty. His voice was deep, resonant, that of a man with self-confidence.

"They're looking for range," Bernie explained, "and I'm trying to talk 'em into buying out Loren Lee."

"Loren wants to sell?" Larkin asked in surprise.

"He could be talked into it."

"Well, it could be a good ranch," Larkin said to the Maxons. "Loren's trouble isn't his range. He just don't know his business."

Zack liked the man at once. If Larkin knew how the Maxons stood in the Piute he gave no sign. He turned down Bernie's invitation to put up his horse and spend the night, saying he had to get home, but he remained to talk a while. From what he said, he knew *his* business inside and out, and Bernie had mentioned earlier that he had made a fine spread out of the old Hawkeye, which was on the north road above Trahan's roadhouse.

"Well, if you decide to set up around here, come and see me," he said before he rode out.

"A fine fellow," Bernie said afterward, "and crazy for Evalyn. But she can't see him."

Zack knew why she could not and wondered if it would be good for her if Ty stayed. But who knew? He was probably taking too much onto his on shoulders, this fearing for Ty, although it was a fear he felt strongly and could not throw off. It had come to him on the old eastbound cattle trail, nine years ago. It was on him strongly as he went to bed, too undecided as to their best course to find quick sleep. He had learned on that drive to Wyoming that the brother he had known as a boy had died on Red Cedar Mountain with their father.

There had been a heavy movement of Shorthorns to Wyoming and eastern Montana to replace the old longhorn breed, finally fallen into disfavor on the vast prairie ranches after ruling the range for so many years. The herd formed on Crooked River, Zack at sixteen its horse wrangler and Ty, at eighteen, old enough to hold down a full riding job.

Yet what Zack remembered most vividly was his own reluctance to tear up his roots again for he had grown to feel at home on Hayfork, where they had found jobs after quitting the Piute. The rancher was a gruff, kindly man who took a fancy to the orphan boys. His wife had been as close to a mother as any woman in Zack's life. But Ty had wanted to trail out with the cattle, the thought of separating from him was worse than leaving Hayfork, so Zack had gone along.

Once they were away from the Crooked, drifting east along the southern flank of the Blues, it had not been so bad. The range up there was less arid, the growth from bunchgrass to yellow pine much heartier, and the country itself was spaciously picturesque. They filed through the Crane Creek mountains, drove finally to the Snake where they made the most dangerous river crossing on all that long drive. Afterward on Idaho's flint-and-sage hills the weather grew hot again, like the Piute Desert, the dry empty wasteland wheeling to all the lonely horizons, and when they passed Boise City the trouble began for them.

It came with a man called Loman, and he was big, vain and rough. The outfit had proved itself inadequate for the rough country, and the trail boss picked up two extra men in the Idaho town. Loman had a cleft chin and surprisingly swift movements for a large man, but it wasn't until Ty pointed it out later that Zack noticed somewhat of a resemblance between him and Sam Milliron.

But even without such a reminder, there would have been friction. Loman liked to belittle the Maxon boys, especially Ty, seeming to resent that he drew the same wages as Loman and did his work even better. He missed no chance to gibe at Ty's youth and lack of experience.

37

Ty was good-natured about it at first, then resentment began to take root in him.

Ty and Zack both had to wear guns, for outlaws ran that country as did the Bannock Indians. The boys knew how to use them well enough to feel no need to prove they could. Loman was proud of his own skill with a shooting iron; he liked to talk about gunslinging exploits and implied that he could relate some of his own. But the explosion did not come for several weeks while the Oregon herd snailed through the Sawtooths, along Camas Prairie, then across the lava desert to the upper Snake close to Blackfoot. There it happened, violently and with an impact that lasted with Ty.

After a night in Blackfoot, Loman was hung over, touchy; breakfast that morning was an uneasy business for all hands, with even the trail boss minding his manners. Maybe Loman had wanted something in the town he failed to get—a fight or a woman—and he still wanted something out of the ordinary that hot, dusty morning.

The camp was only half broken, bedding lying about, a sage fire still burning under the old black coffee pot, the chuckwagon's tailgate still down and cluttered. It was a requirement that the riders roll their beds and carry them to the wagon before they saddled for the day's drive—under penalty of having them left where they lay by the cook—and Ty had half rolled his bed before the cook banged his dishpan and announced breakfast.

When he had eaten, Loman tossed aside his plate, rose and started toward the rope corral where Zack was holding the remuda for the day's mount. Instead of taking a few steps around Ty's bed, Loman walked across it. A spur caught in a blanket, jerking it after him.

Turning with a bitter curse, Loman began to kick the bed, deliberately scattering Ty's belongings in his efforts to free his foot. Ty came upright like the blade of a spring knife. That only inspired in Loman a final kick that sent the blankets scudding across the dirt.

"Loman," Ty said in a low, flat voice, "put that bed back the way it was."

Loman gave him an amused sneer and started on toward the horses.

"Loman!"

When the man swung around he saw something neither

38

he nor any of them had ever seen in Ty Maxon. The youth was gone, an ageless fury standing on Ty's face and shaping the intense lines of his body. Loman stared at him with bright, interested eyes, startled by that intensity, driven to disdain of it. The trail boss flung a helpless, pleading look at Ty, trying to save him from himself, from his inexperienced folly. Zack, standing by the horses, knew with benumbed certainty that in another minute Ty would be dead. Loman was building to that as he watched Ty, silent and thoughtful. He wasn't altogether a bluff.

"I'm counting three," Ty said.

Loman pulled in a breath, disbelief breaking the hard set of his face when Ty said, "One." His shoulders began a slight, slow rise at the count of, "Two—" and then Loman's streaking hand fisted his gun and the gun roared out.

He was dead before he hit the ground.

Nausea boiled in Zack's stomach as he watched. Ty was as old as time standing there with a smoke-dribbling pistol in his hand, and a second thing had happened to change him and his life. The trail boss broke a sick silence to say, "Well, if anybody ever asked for it, he did." Then they were bending over Loman, and Ty was holstering his gun. Zack fought to keep his nausea from gushing out.

The sheriff saw it as the trail outfit did, and Ty wasn't held. His only comment to Zack afterward was when he mentioned Loman's resemblence to Sam Milliron, almost as if he had destroyed Milliron instead of Loman. Zack began to understand why this earlier wrath had centered on Milliron. There had been other men on Red Cedar, but Sam Milliron had somehow personalized the issue by doing the shouting at Kelsey. The force of this had driven his image deeper into Ty's mind. There, where the lesion still lay unhealed, it had focussed Ty's rage, and this had found a temporary outlet in the dead Loman.

The herd was delayed three days. Then it trailed on, Ty's status changed, with Zack coming in for some of the men's awe because he was Ty's brother and like him in several ways. The Snake was put behind, the Oregon cattle filing up the Blackfoot River, through Star Valley and on into western Wyoming. It threaded South Pass, passed down the Sweetwater and then the Platte and was delivered

39

to a ranch on the La Bone, where the trail hands were paid off.

Before the herd reached Wyoming, Wad Piper, who had signed on with Loman at Boise City, had transferred his admiration to Ty, who accepted it with less indifference than Zack liked. Ty rode night herd with Piper, and Zack knew they talked a lot about matters in line with the drifter's natural interests. A fast gunhand always attracted that kind of following, and the followers often were the ones full of ideas as to how such an adroitness could be made to pay dividends.

There had been no agreement but Zack had held the hope that, when they were off the drive, Ty and he would go back to Hayfork. But Ty wanted to see Cheyenne, and when he had done so he wanted to accompany Piper to Deadwood, and so they had drifted into the worst winter ever to hit the prairie ranges, Wad Piper still with them.

They holed up in Deadwood, the kind of wide-open town Ty and Piper liked where Ty finished maturing, learning about women, liquor and cards, and their money went fast. Piper was lucky or deft with cards and made a little that way, always ready to share his winnings. So Ty wasn't worried, but Zack couldn't help but be. Moreover, the mining camp and blizzard-harassed Hills bored and wore on him, engendering a constant longing for the open country.

Then one night in a poker game Piper was killed. The man who shot him, and the others in the game, swore he had been caught cheating. Ty took it up, dropping a hint that the man had better find new diggings. Zack knew then that the combination of Loman and Piper had turned him into what Piper had wanted him to be. The threatened man took the advice and left; another crisis was turned aside, but a third thing had happened to set the course of Ty's life.

Cattle were dying everywhere on the northern ranges that winter and early spring. From Montana deep into Colorado, snow, ice and sub-zero temperatures destroyed herd after herd, and conditions were especially bad on the bare plains outside the Hills. But Zack struck out, leaving it to Ty to follow, using the only power he had against Ty's deadly new drive—the strong affection that had always held them together. Ty caught up with him at Buffalo

40

Gap. They drifted on through the storm to Sidney, Zack hoping they would go back to Hayfork at last although now, broke, they would have to ride a freight.

Instead they were offered jobs with the Union Cattle Company, which was hiring riders to throw back their cattle from the river to which the storm pushed them and where they soon starved to death. It was the hardest work of Zack's life, but he did it, turning seventeen that spring, in every other respect a full-grown man. Ty kept calling him a kid, but Zack was the one thereafter who bore a sense of responsibility he had never since been able to cast off.

After the Chinook, which came in late March, there was plenty of work to be had. Many of the smaller outfits and some of the big ones had gone down under the onslaughts of the winter, but many—soundly financed and managed—were able to restock their ranges. In effect there was a larger movement than ever of cattle being brought in. The Maxon brothers went to Texas with an outfit and came back to Nebraska. The Union people kept them on, the Nebraska range boss taking a liking to Zack although he never warmed to Ty.

They made another drive from the Umatilla, in Oregon, and by then Zack liked his new job and had lost his homesickness for Hayfork. Ty quit that fall and was gone until the next summer. He became like Kelsey, explaining his movements vaguely or with patent distortions of the truth or not at all. He attracted other Wad Pipers—it didn't matter what the name was, the men were much the same —and they would take him off. Yet he always came back to Zack in the end to work through a roundup with Union, never resenting it that Zack was making progress with the company. He always had money, more than Zack ever managed to save from his wages.

When Zack wakened in his bedroom in the old Quick ranchhouse the memories that had streamed through his mind in the night had left him with a decision. He had thrown up eight years of work with Union at a time when he was ready to step into a top range job, because his choice had been that or a permanent break with Ty. He was not a man to look back on that with bitterness, and he did not regret it if it would help Ty find himself.

He knew that Ty valued freedom above all else, as Kelsey had; that if he ever stuck with anything it would have to be something that would arouse in him a personal responsibility and pride of possession, like a ranch of their own. Perhaps it didn't matter so much where it was. The last happiness Ty had known had been here on the Piute; here he might have the best chance to find it again.

6

Years ago Basque sheepherders came across the Sierras from the great valley of California with bands of sheep to winter on the white sage around the desert, then move into the Garnets as spring opened and the high ranges cleared. A one-room adobe house had been built by them at the base of the Garnets and here, now that cattle had taken over the country, Loren Lee lived alone. Around eight o'clock, because he wanted to catch Lee before he rode out on his day's work, Bernie Quick came over the low ridge east of the place, feeling pleasantly stirred by the prospect of putting Lee in the mood to sell out.

That morning Zack had thrown in the towel, as Bernie and Ty had expected he would, and Bernie had suggested that—in view of the circumstances—it might be better for him to approach Lee about the deal by himself. Both the Maxon boys had proved themselves better heeled than Bernie had expected; he would offer Lee a good price to speed things up, although the price was really of little consequence considering a certain thought in Bernie's head.

Lee's place would make a good line camp, he thought contemptuously as he stared down through the heat at the house, its sagging corrals and sheds, and the patched, rusting old windmill that creaked in chronic complaint above a dirty tank. The trouble all along the base of the Garnets, he reflected, with Michaels and Newkirk as well as Lee, was a beaten acceptance of the hands they had been dealt by life, and an abject willingness to go on year after year, buffeted by the weather, the cattle market, taking things as they were or as they came.

Bernie didn't believe in submissiveness. It had affected his father, with the result that Thurm had taken out his frustrations and disappointments with a tug strap on his son. Bernie would always carry the scars and under the scars a callousness that never again would know human feeling. He didn't consider himself any smarter than other men; there were too many things that bewildered him. But he had this protective cover that he shared with Ty Maxon —men of that nature seemed to sense it in each other—a lightning, lashing deadliness. He was also trapwise and trap wary, and when he had done all he could to determine events, he had enough fatalism to accept what could not be avoided, evaded or overcome.

He was thinking of the weakness of Lee, to say nothing of the fear that must be worming in him now that the Maxons had arrived, and he was confident of using it to gain his end. He was thinking also of Jake Michaels, who had a weakness even more easily exploited if a man wanted to use it.

Michaels was clean gone on Daycie Newkirk. She was probably thirty years younger than her husband Ben, and when he liked to go to sleep at nightfall she liked to slip out the back door to meet Jake. Ben was the type of man who wouldn't suspect anything unless he fell over them in the dark, and if that ever happened he was the kind that would blow off Michaels' head on the spot.

Lee came to the steps as Bernie rode on in, and his thin, under-sized face showed concern through its whiskers. His hair was shaggy, uncombed, and he had probably just got out of bed since industry in the dawn was something Lee looked upon with disfavor. He did not often attract visitors unless they came with some complaint or to ask his help in some pesky job no one else would help with, and on rare occasions when there was some kind of community emergency.

Bernie saw the apprehension in the man and tipped a curt nod as he reined in and swung out of the saddle. Lee waited by the door, expecting him to speak, and Bernie let him wait as he moved toward the steps.

"You're out early," Lee said, inviting an explanation of this visit.

43

"Before breakfast," Bernie agreed coolly. "You ate yet?"

"Just did. But come on in."

Lee relaxed a little, assuming that if his unexpected guest had anything alarming in mind he would not be thinking of his belly. Bernie followed the puny rancher into the house, privately wrinkling his nose at its unclean clutter. Lee poured him some coffee, greased the stove top and ladled three flat pools of hotcake batter onto the smoking surface. Bernie took a seat at the table and pushed a space clear in front of him. He was pleasantly relaxed because he knew already that this was going to be easy.

Lee, waiting while the hotcakes cooked, kept swinging his head to look at his visitor. He grew more and more nervous in his anxiety to know what was coming but thought he wasn't showing it. He lifted the cakes onto a cracked plate and placed them before Bernie, then shooed the flies from a sticky syrup pitcher. Bernie poured syrup over the cakes.

"Did you hear the Maxon boys are back?" he asked as he pushed the edge of a fork through the stack and began to eat.

Lee's body jerked. He went to the stove again, poured coffee for himself, came back to the table and sat down weakly.

"Yeah, I heard," he said. "What are they doing here?"

"Looking for a ranch."

"Here?" Lee straightened the slump of his shoulders.

"Right here on old Piute. They're interested in my place."

"Oh, Jesus," Lee muttered.

Bernie gave him a look of mock surprise. "What's the matter? Don't you want them for next-door neighbors?"

"Not me," Lee said, shoving to his feet. He walked to the stove, swung and came back empty-handed. "Look here—you don't mean that, do you?"

"We all but closed the deal last night."

"If you sell to them, I ain't staying here."

Bernie lifted an eyebrow. "You're thinking about that old trouble."

"You're damned right I am. They haven't forgotten that little business. They'd ride me rough, with Michaels and Newkirk coming in for the same thing. My life wouldn't be worth a plugged nickel, and neither would their's."

44

Bernie failed to see where Lee's was worth that much as it was. The man lived like a Digger, had no real friends, no woman would look at him, and misfortune seemed to dog his life.

"Well, I don't really want to sell," Bernie said. "I'm just attracted by the money they're offering. But if I don't sell, Loren, Michaels or Newkirk would. The Maxons want on the Piute and are ready to pay what they have to to get on."

"Now," Lee said irritably, "why do they want on the Piute that bad?"

"Maybe they figure things weren't settled up there on Red Cedar, like you said. Could be they aim to take their own sweet time about balancing the books."

Lee made a nervous turn around the floor. "Sure as hell," he agreed. "That's what they're up to."

"You ever consider selling out, Loren?"

"No, but if they're buying, you can bet I'm selling."

"But who'd buy your place?" Bernie asked scornfully.

"I could find somebody," Lee said defensively. He paced to the door where he swung, suddenly excited. "Say, maybe they'd buy this outfit. There ain't a thing wrong with it that money wouldn't fix. That's been my trouble. Hardly a pot to piddle in, and a man can't build up a ranch like that."

"I'm not sure I don't want that deal, myself."

"Look," Lee said desperately, "you can get along with 'em. You were always close friends. They'd kill me and do it slow. I always knew they'd come back and when they did me and Jake and Ben would pay through our noses. Sam Milliron, too. He figures he's a few notches above the rest of us, but he was in on that and everybody knows it."

"What kind of a price would you want?" Bernie said uncertainly.

"I'd make 'em a good price. Ten dollars range count for the steers, five for the cows, calves and buildings thrown in. I'd keep my horses, that's all."

Bernie doubted if the spread was worth that to a man without Lee's attachment. Yet the price didn't really matter, the thing was to get Lee anxious to sell out. When a man bought a ranch he acquired little in fee simple but the stock and installations. The main gain here would be the grazing rights that would go with the deal.

45

"Well," he said thoughtfully, "I see your fix. I wouldn't want to live next to them two if I'd shot Kelsey Maxon."

"I didn't shoot him!" Lee cried. "That was Jake Michaels! Maxon made a run for it, finally, and Jake dropped him!"

Bernie's eyes glinted. "I always wondered," he said.

"Why don't you tell 'em that?" Lee urged, anxious to turn the lightning away from himself.

Bernie gave him a contemptuous glance. "It wouldn't save you, Loren. You were all in on it—All there to hang him, and that's what they remember."

"Where you going if you sell out?"

"Never thought that far."

"Look!" Lee said in sudden excitement. "Here's a real deal. Take their fancy price, and I'll let you have this one for next to nothing. There's a fat profit for you, and it'd get me off the hook."

"Now, maybe you've got something there," Bernie mused.

"You wouldn't have to leave the Piute," Lee pointed out, "if that's what's been holding you back on their offer. Why don't we go into Piute and see that lawyer—Weatherby—and have him draw up the papers. Don't let the Maxons know about it, and you can send me my money when you've got yours from them."

"You'll sell Michaels and Newkirk down the river if I'll doublecross the Maxons. Is that it?"

"I don't give a damn about Jake and Ben, and I don't reckon you're worried about the Maxons."

"Not a damned bit," Bernie admitted. "All right, Loren. Let's go to town."

"I'll get ready," Lee said in enormous relief.

Bernie knew he was too frightened to see the loopholes in what had been said, was aware of nothing as yet but his own chance to escape. The thing had to be wound up in an ironclad manner before the panic left him. But Bernie had come prepared. Before leaving home he had secured from Ty two thousand in cash, which Lee would accept gladly and which also would make the transaction thoroughly aboveboard. It would be a cash purchase; he would make a point of paying Lee in the lawyer's presence. Lee might begin to understand then that the whole thing was contrived, but his fear of the Maxons and possession

46

of the money would decide him to let well enough alone.

They reached Piute just after the noon hour. Frank Weatherby was in his law office; he listened to the terms and drew up the papers. They were signed and notarized, Bernie counted out the purchase price in currency and gold eagles. Lee's eyes bugged, but he didn't speak until they were on the street again.

"How come you were packing that kind of money?" he asked.

"I was in Virginia City, last week, and my luck ran sweet," Bernie said easily. "And I don't trust banks."

"I don't either," Lee said. "Risky to carry that much money, but I reckon I'll keep it on me."

Bernie smiled. The man meant to quit the country as soon as he picked up his horses and personal possessions.

They rode across the hot neck of the desert together, but Bernie left Lee where the cut-off from the Garnets came in, continuing on along the stage road. He had a deed to the new range in his pocket, and the next step was a partnership with Ty and Zack. With the acquisition, the old Quick ranch had more than doubled in range, and already Bernie felt a pride of possession he had never known before. Zack knew more about ranching than he and Ty put together, and they would let him take the lead. The brothers still had money for additional cattle, and there was plenty more range in the Piute.

He reached home to find that Zack had saddled a horse at noon and ridden off someplace, Ty thought just for a ride, and it suited Bernie as well to have this chance to speak to Ty alone. Except to ask about Zack, he didn't say anything until they were in the house and he had got out a bottle. He poured whisky, seeing from Ty's brightening eyes that he knew the effort had brought results.

Bernie picked up a glass and said, "To the new cattle firm of Maxon and Quick. The MQ—don't that sound good?"

"So it worked."

"Like shooting fish in a barrel." Bernie pulled out the deed and showed it to Ty. "It cost you the two thousand and a bargain considering how the cat can come back." He laughed.

"Where'll Lee head?" Ty asked.

"The one way he can go the quickest without seeing

47

anybody he knows. He'll make for the closest California town on the S. P., and to do that he'll have to go through Mosquito Pass in the Garnets."

"When?"

"He won't risk it before dark. Don't worry about that."

They drank the toast but were too excited to need extra stimulation. Ty said Zack had drawn a little over three thousand out of a Cheyenne bank and he had another two thousand himself. Bernie would have three to four thousand worth of beef to sell that fall, and if the cat came home as expected there'd be that two thousand more. Holding something back to run on, they could buy five hundred young cows across the line in Oregon as soon as they could be brought in. The MQ was a going concern, already.

Bernie had enough horses because he loved them and had really had too many when it was a one-man ranch. They would weed out Lee's worst stuff at roundup to keep it from wasting grass, get the new steers in and settled on the bunchgrass and the white sage that, after the first heavy frost, sends up nourishing shoots the cattle liked. If winter held off long enough they might even get in a wild horse hunt. Once it socked in, if ranch work wasn't too heavy, they might make a trip to the Comstock and have some fun there.

Finally, Bernie said, "I found out who shot your dad. Lee blurted it out. It was Jake Michaels."

After a long moment, Ty said, "That's the best thing you've said yet."

7

Sam Milliron had tried to tell himself that the return of the Maxons meant nothing in his life, but he knew it did. Red Cedar Mountain obsessed his thoughts, time kept rolling backward and forcing him to live that period over and over again. It had been several days since Nancy told

48

him of seeing Zack at the old cabin, and that according to Evalyn they were back only for a short visit. So far they had made no trouble. That seemed to show they meant no harm, in a few days they would leave, and this suspense would be put behind. But Sam couldn't believe it would pass away that easily and that soon.

It seemed far less than ten years since the sheriff rode into this very ranchyard where Sam sat brooding, a sternness on him that told Sam immediately something was very wrong. Then the truth had come out; a renegade down from the Oregon desert had stolen the Michaels horses and been caught going home with them. Had anyone but Kelsey Maxon been involved in the gunfight on the mountain the rest of them would have been in deep trouble then and there. As it was, the case was dropped, but that was of little consequence to Sam for the real penalties had been inflicted inside him. The extenuating circumstances that kept them from trouble with the law had no effect on his feelings.

His outfit was the most prosperous on the Piute, next in size to the Hames ranch on the Roaring Horse and Vince Meyer's RC on Rye Creek. He had been the first to take up land in the spring-watered low hills between Red Cedar and the Garnets, and those had been wild times. The closest civilization had been the Comstock mining region far to the south, and up here it had been necessary to make law and administer it according to need and the means at hand. Many a horse and cattle thief had been hung on capture, and that had been a judical expedient everyone accepted, excepting perhaps the thieves. So what they had done in the Maxon case had seemed natural and justified. Even when the mistake was revealed, few had really blamed them.

The Milliron ranchhouse lay in the morning shadows of Red Cedar and in the afternoon old willows and cottonwoods growing along Antelope Creek kept it well shaded. Like most ranchers in summer, Sam spent his leisure on the covered porch. As he sat there smoking his pipe after the noon meal, he began to wonder if Nancy—who was cleaning up in the kitchen—condemned him for what he had helped do that fateful night. She was plainly worried and more than once Sam had suspected that her turmoil

49

involved more than fear, that it was primarily a deep-going reproach of him.

She came out presently, her work done until it was time to start supper. He saw her restlessness as she went to the edge of the porch and looked out through the trees, and he knew she was wondering what to do with the next few hours. It was a pity she had not had brothers and sisters, but none had come along, then her mother had died and Sam had not felt like marrying again.

"Why don't you take a run into town?" he suggested.

She shook her head. "I was in just the other day, and the desert's so hot now. Anyway, Piute's repulsive since the railroad came."

"It's booming this part of the country, though," Sam said, eager for something practical and reassuring to talk about. "It's hard to get used to the fact, but we're not so cut off anymore." He saw that the thought had no effect on her and admitted that nothing would ever relieve the isolation of the Piute, or fill its emptiness or tame its wildness, that the new activity in town was carnal in the main and offensive to a fastidious girl like Nancy. "Why don't you go up to see Evalyn?" he added.

"The Maxon boys are around there quite a bit, and I don't want to run into them."

"They've got nothing against you," he said tartly.

"I just don't want to see them." Nancy turned and went back into the house.

Sam was irritated by her moodiness although he was by nature a congenial, contented man. Noticing that his pipe had gone out, he tamped down the half-burned to-bacco with a calloused finger and applied a match. He knew that he had been affected by his many years on the desert, that changes had been made in him as they were made in all desert creatures. This undoubtedly had made him less companionable than a woman liked, even less admirable. A man could get used to emptiness and ferocity and—at least the young ones—could find excitement in the crude earthiness of its people and the raw new rail town.

Yet some of the changes wrought in him would once have offended him if he had known they were to come. He had been rendered aimless beyond the grim necessities of survival and physical well-being. He was less sure of

50

himself and the meaning of a man's life than he had once been. He had grown a protective shell just as a mesquite or cactus grew one. He had learned to strike out when he had to do it, to avoid unnecessary trouble, and to accept disaster as a daily possibility.

Physically a large man with greying sandy hair, a strong face with a cleft chin, he was still hale at fifty-five, and the stray thought passed through his mind that he could still marry if for no other reason than to provide company for Nancy. He knew at once that the idea was ridiculous. The only eligible woman of his age on the Piute was Mamma Trahan, and he disliked her thoroughly.

He was saddling a horse when he saw Jake Michaels coming and from the way Jake rode he knew something was wrong. He finished the chore but had not swung up when Michaels thundered into the yard, spotted him and hauled up at the corral in a fold of dust.

"Jesus, Sam," Jake gasped.

"What's wrong, man?"

"They got Loren Lee."

"Killed him?" Sam rapped out. "Who?"

Michaels lifted both hands in desperation. "Who would it be but the Maxon boys?"

Words kept spilling out of him like charged water from a shaken bottle. Two Alta men going through Mosquito Pass had found Lee there and brought him back to Michaels' place. Lee had been shot five times, receiving the contents of a sixgun, apparently. His horse had drifted off a ways, so stealing it hadn't been the reason, and it bore a saddle roll with Lee's personals in it. That showed he had been leaving on a trip, and his body had had a money belt around it containing nothing.

"Robbery, sure as hell," Sam said. "Where do the Maxons come in?"

"Hell, they rigged it to look like a holdup," Michaels said with conviction. "It didn't take all them slugs to kill Loren, which makes it pure spite. We're next, Sam—you and me and old Ben."

"Get hold of yourself, damn it," Sam said, although he was shaken. "There's so much scum in this country now it could have been anybody. Lee was going into hiding till the Maxons leave—I allow that. So he had money on him. Met somebody, they saw he was traveling and smelled

51

the money. And some of them like to empty a gun—the vicious stripe."

"I'm going for the sheriff," Michaels said. "And he'll track the thing to the Maxons, you wait and see."

"That's what you hope," Sam said bitterly. "But if they're on the prod, he won't cut it in time to save us. But I don't see it your way, anyhow not yet."

Michaels was widely built but not tall. His hair was heavy, a flat black, and the stubble he usually wore was thick and wiry. His coarse, mundane mentality made his eyes bright instead of dull, for some reason, so that he seemed to possess the untamed virility of a wild stallion. Michaels stared in his glittering, wary way at Sam, then rode out, heading for the Piute telegraph office.

Sam's horse started from habit as he rode to the saddle, but Sam had no idea now where he was going. Swinging the horse into the shade of the willow behind the house he sat staring at the blank side of his blacksmith shop. Nobody cared about Loren Lee, but he had been one of them and it was indeed strange that he should die violently while the Maxon boys were here on what they called a visit. Yet Sam didn't want to believe it was more than coincidence. All the men in the Piute owned money belts, being so far from a bank. Lee's wearing one only meant that he had been going into hiding, and the robber could not have got much for his trouble.

All at once Sam knew what he had to do. The only way to clear the atmosphere was to ride over to Bernie Quick's and see the Maxons, if they were there, or try to learn from Bernie whether they had something stuck in their craws. All through his life when he had something difficult to face he had done it promptly, knowing that courage could drain out of a man like blood from an open vein.

He rode out, heading slightly west of south, presently crossing the north road and going on across country. The day's heat was rising to its fullest, its burning light lending the effect of fire and smoke to the tawny hills. He was halfway to the old TQ headquarters before it dawned on him that he hadn't brought a gun, then he laughed sourly at himself. If they wanted to kill him a gun would only invite that result. He went on.

He admitted as he put distance behind that he had always resented Kelsey Maxon, as an accepting, conforming

52

man distrusts and dislikes those who rebel against the well-grooved ways of life. It had always irritated him to think of Kelsey up there on Red Cedar, free as a bird, doing as he pleased, owning nothing and therefore spared the worries that were so much a part of Sam Milliron's life. It had been easy to grow suspicious of a man like that, to let suspicion become conviction—to act.

He came around the final butte to see before him across the flat meadow the huddle of the Quick headquarters, marked as on all the ranches by old trees, the only shade except that thrown by the hills when the sun hung low to the horizon. He felt his muscles tighten but rode on steadily, seeing as he neared that there were no horses about the house, although Bernie's big saddle band was scattered in the pasture. The empty corral suggested that no one was home. That at first relieved him, then he felt disappointment for he wanted to know where he stood. He rode on in to be sure, then to his surprise saw a big, red-headed man sitting on the porch smoking a cigarette. He looked like a total stranger except for his hair, which told Sam who he was.

Sam rode up to the porch and tipped an uncertain nod. "I reckon you're Zack," he said without preamble. His uneasiness left, now that he had met it. He sat quietly and with dignity, waiting.

Zack nodded and rose to his feet and came to the edge of the porch. If he recognized the visitor he didn't show it. His eyes were reserved, appraising, although his manner seemed courteous.

"Bernie ain't home?" Sam asked.

Shaking his head, Zack said, "I guess you're Sam Milliron. You've changed, yourself."

"I'm older," Sam said. "Your brother here?"

"They went over to Trahan's."

"It was one of you boys I wanted to see, anyhow. Mind if I light down?"

"Light," Zack said.

Sam stepped down from the horse, dropped the reins and walked onto the porch, mindful of the fact that if the Maxons wanted him, Zack had him now. When he had taken one of the chairs and pulled off his hat to cool his head, he let out a long breath. Zack sat down, silent, waiting.

53

"To get to the point," Sam said, "you boys probably hate the sight of me. But considering what's happened the last day or two, I want to know how it's to be between you and me."

"Why, what's happened?" Zack asked.

"Somebody killed Loren Lee last night in Mosquito Pass."

"Lee?" Zack said incredulously.

There was no acting there. The man's rugged face looked shocked. Sam knew in that moment he had had nothing to do with it and was vastly relieved. But he had asked his question and still wanted to know how big a grudge they carried against him.

"Are you sure of that?" Zack asked.

Sam told him about Michaels and what Jake had reported, concluding, "Some trail wolf, probably. Smelled money."

"There *was* money," Zack said. "Bernie bought Lee out yesterday."

"Well, I'll be damned. Lee was carrying cash?"

"I don't know, but that's the way Bernie paid him. Somebody knew Lee had it and laid for him."

Suspiciously, Sam said, "What does Bernie want with Lee's outfit?"

"He was buying it partly for us. We're going partners with him."

"You're going to stay here?"

"That's right. You asked a question, Milliron, and you've got a right to the answer. It was a hell of a thing you men did on Red Cedar Mountain. If I said I liked it, I'd sound like a lunatic. But it never made me hate anybody enough to kill him, let alone go through his pockets."

Sam looked earnestly into Zack's face. It was strong, the eyes were level, the mouth was neither too hard nor too soft. The voice was pleasant, the manner courteous, and if a man didn't know the connection he would see little to remind him of the father. Sam remembered that the younger boy had always been the one he liked the better, or perhaps disliked the less. Now he found it impossible to be afraid of him.

"I'm glad you're not looking for trouble," Sam said. "You're right that it was a bad thing we did that night. You've got every reason to resent it, and I'm not begging

54

off when I tell you it's been the big regret of my life. If I could undo it, I would. Since I can't, I've got to live with it. I always got along with Bernie, although there's little liking between us. I'll do my part to get along with you boys."

"That's fair enough, Milliron."

"You going to get more cattle?" Sam asked and, at Zack's nod, went on, "I heard of a good buy the other day. Woman up on the Malheur lost her husband and wants to sell out."

"How big's the herd?"

"Couple of thousand, everything counted. But the price is low because she's in a hurry."

"Too big," Zack said. "We figured on five hundred head to start. But thanks for the tip."

Nodding, Sam walked out to his horse, rose to saddle and headed home. His relief was enormous and, oddly enough, he had been favorably impressed by Zack Maxon. He had all but forgotten what had happened to Loren Lee. The man had been one of the eyesores of the desert, spineless, shiftless, with no qualities to inspire liking. Sam could form his own idea of what had happened in the pass. Lee was inclined to strut when he had a little in his pocket, and he had picked the wrong man for an audience. That cut-off into California had as many passersby as the north road, and a lot of them stopped at Lee's well.

When Sam reached home the afternoon was about gone, and he put up his horse. Nancy was seated on the porch, and he wanted to cheer her up. Dropping his hat on the floor as he sat down with her he gave her the first smile that had formed on his face since he heard of the Maxons' return.

"Just seen Zack," he said, "and, do you know, that man's all right."

Nancy looked at him with sharpened interest. "What do you base that conclusion on?"

"His looks, the way he acts. Bernie's bought out Lee, and they're buying into it."

"They're staying here?" Nancy gasped.

"Moreover, somebody killed Lee in the pass last night and took the money."

"They did it," Nancy said instantly.

Sam shook his head. "I can be wrong sometimes, but

55

this time I'm not. It was sure a surprise to Zack. I'll confess I've been worried about that pair. When I heard about
Lee I figured I'd better ask for the showdown myself. So
I did. He was the only one there, and he sure isn't looking
for trouble."

"How about Ty? And Bernie? I don't know Ty, but I
sure do know Bernie."

Giving her a sharp look, Sam said, "Some day you'll
learn not to judge men so fast. The way I had to learn it."

The hostility left her face and she said, "I know. It
must have been hard for you to go over to face them."

"Easier than waiting for them to bring trouble to me."

8

Zack Maxon had a strange feeling as he watched Sam
Milliron ride out. His mind had not yet fully accepted the
fact that Loren Lee was dead, that Milliron had at once
suspected him and Ty. He had an idea he had put the
suspicion out of the man's mind, but everyone else on the
Piute was going to harbor it. He had gone to bed shortly
after dark the night before and as was his habit had fallen
at once into a deep, unbroken sleep that lasted until dawn.
He wouldn't let his mind reach to the question trying to
form as to whether Ty and Bernie had done the same.

Why wouldn't they have? If Ty had wanted to kill Loren
Lee he would have done it face to face in a fight. He
would not have stooped to robbery at the same time. Even
so, they were both in for rough going from the sheriff
because of that old enmity. All they could do was insist
they hadn't been off the ranch all night, which might not
hold water with anybody.

Unless they catch the right man again, he thought bitterly, and in time . . .

It was a rotten thing to happen when the situation had
begun to look good. That morning he had talked with Ty
and Bernie, made plans. He was convinced that they were

both in dead earnest about building up the new MQ iron. They were restless men—but they knew cattle and had enough sense to separate work from play. From the start they would be sure of a living with prospects of doing much better. They were young while their neighbors were getting on in years, so there were possibilities of buying more range in time. Eventually this might let them break up into separate ranches so he could have his own. That was what he really wanted for he was by nature a family man. If only Evalyn—Zack shook his head. As long as Ty was around she was out of reach.

Ty and Bernie came in just as Zack was starting a supper fire. Zack told them about Milliron's visit, what Sam had revealed about Loren Lee.

"I'll be go to hell," Bernie commented. "Well, I don't see how it could void the land deal. That was all wrapped up in the lawyer's office, and Weatherby saw Loren get paid."

"It won't affect the sale," Ty said. He seemed indifferent, as if he had forgotten completely that Lee was one of the men who had been on Red Cedar Mountain.

"Just the same," Zack said tartly, "we're going to get raked over the coals about it."

"I doubt it," Bernie answered. "Lee was the kind of man you had to think twice to remember. Which made him never miss a chance to show off when he was feeling prosperous. This time it cost him his worthless life. As long as it don't upset the deal, forget it."

The sheriff was there around noon the next day. He was a new man and his name was Webster. He apparently had got a considerable briefing already from Jake Michaels, who had sent for him, and Michaels' opinions were positive. He had been to the pass, Webster said, but the road carried too much traffic for him to determine anything definite.

"So," he concluded, "you boys will have to explain what you were doing last night."

"Look," Ty said easily. "Michaels don't know yet that the three of us here bought Lee out. He was probably carrying two thousand in cash, and there's your motive. You can check with Weatherby in town. He handled the deal."

"You bought Lee out?" the sheriff said, his pale eyes narrowing. "That's a motive, but it still don't clear you

57

Maxons. Who would know better than you that Lee had the money on him? And you still haven't said what you were doing last night."

"Up to bed time," Ty said, "we were here talking business. Then we turned in."

"Nobody happened along to see you here?"

"No."

"Can any of you say the other two were here all night?"

"Was it two men?" Bernie asked.

"Signs of that. They fouled the trail, which was easy up there, but it looks like they turned back onto the desert instead of going on into California. Well, I had to check with you. If there's anything else, I'll let you know."

"Say," Bernie said, "was Lee driving horses?"

"There was too much traffic up there to tell. Why?"

"I just happened to think of something. The only thing he held back was his horses. Said he was going to take them with him. And there's your answer. Some damned horse thieves knocked him off for the horses, found the money on him and took it."

"That sounds reasonable," Webster said, nodding. After a little casual talk, he rode out.

"Thank God you remembered that," Ty said. "We were sure on the hook."

"He was anxious to button the thing up," Bernie answered. "That does it, and you can relax. Now, when are we going to buy some more steers?"

Zack felt an enormous relief, not only because the sheriff had been satisfied but because there was a plausible enough explanation for what had happened to Lee to put down his own suspicions. Anxious to think of less somber things, he said, "Milliron told me about a good buy, but it's too big for us. Two thousand head, up on the Malheur. Somebody died and his wife wants to get out from under quick."

"I've been up that way," Bernie said. "Did Sam say who it was?"

Zack shook his head. "It's not likely the woman would cut the herd up for us, anyway."

"Maybe we could handle it all."

"How? Even if we had the range, it would take at least twenty thousand to swing a deal that big."

"As for range," Bernie said promptly, "we could pasture

58

what we couldn't handle in the vegas east of Red Cedar till shipping time. There's three outfits over there that're all understocked, and they'd be glad to get pasturage fees. Then look where we'd be. We could take the pick for brood stock and ship the rest."

"That takes care of everything," Zack said, "except the money to buy the herd."

"We've got some, and the rest we could get at the bank. Let's go see Sam and find out more about that herd. A forced sale like that don't come along very often."

Zack agreed that it sounded like a rare opportunity; even Sam Milliron had thought so. There were advantages in what Bernie suggested, and few cattle outfits operated without outside financing. It was probable that they could farm out the stuff they could not range themselves. There was nothing to suggest a shaky market that fall, and the outcome could well be a neat profit, as well as an upgraded cow herd for future increase. He was tempted, and it was at least worth looking into, in spite of his feeling that they were moving too fast. Bernie and Ty were gamblers, he decided, while he was not, and they had their rights, too.

When they came to the north road just above Milliron's, Bernie said, "Why don't we kill two birds with one rock? You go get the dope from Sam, Zack, and Ty and me'll ride on over the mountain and see Frank Ashton about pasture. We won't commit ourselves, just find out."

Zack agreed and turned south. It was then midafternoon and with the brassy sun at the end of Red Cedar its whole green-swept side was brilliantly lighted. It was a pleasant sight to him, lying as all the formations in this country did like a great, sleeping lizard on the flat desert floor. There were signs everywhere in this corner of the state that once the entire country had been a vast lake in which some of the larger mountains had been islands, producing a striking contrast of glassy flatness and sudden upthrusts.

When he rode in to the Milliron house, it hardly seemed that ten years had slipped away since he had been there last. He came in among the old trees to see a girl alone on the porch. She watched him curiously, then he thought she stiffened, perhaps guessing who he was. She had risen to her feet when he rode up to the porch, and his impression was confirmed that she was very pretty.

59

"You must be Nancy," he said, pulling off his hat.

"Hello, Zack." Her voice was reserved, cool.

"Your father home?"

"He went to Piute, this morning." She started to say more, then hesitated, and he saw curiosity at work in her, tangling with a natural antagonism toward him. Part of that came from the fact that he was a man of uncertain reputation and she a woman alone on a ranch. But as she watched him he saw her expression soften, just as Sam's had when he came over to Quick's. Apparently she wasn't finding him as bad as she had expected.

He said, "He told me yesterday about a herd for sale up north, and I wanted more details."

Puzzling a moment, Nancy said, "That must be the Belkirk cattle. I heard somebody tell him about it in Piute the other day. It may have been sold by now, though."

"Do you know where they are? I could send a wire and see."

"The ranch is close to a town called Juntura on the Malheur."

"I know where that is. And the name's Belkirk. Thanks."

He picked up his reins, and as he started to take his leave he saw something troubled in her eyes, her cheeks coloring as she glanced away. Wondering about him, he knew, what kind of a man he had become. Maybe she did not accept the fact that he was not back for revenge against her father and the others. He touched his hat and left.

When he reached the place where the weed-grown road switched off for the mountain, he realized that he had been cooped up so much the last couple of days he was not attracted by the idea of returning at once to the ranch. He decided to ride onto Red Cedar and maybe keep going until he met Ty and Bernie coming back from the Ashton outfit, which lay out on the desert on the east side.

He took the old road, the horse soon beginning the steep climb up the blunt side of the great *cuesta,* and as he came to the top he had a sudden feeling of the freedom he had known up here as a boy. He wondered why a man had to lose so much of himself that was good, why he must busy himself for most of his life striving for goals half understood and often disappointing when attained.

60

Once on top he could see the fresh tracks of the two horses preceding him, enabled to tell by the way the forepart of the prints sank deeper than the rest that Ty and Bernie had let their mounts slope out. He grinned, feeling something of the old boyhood affection for that hellion pair. He had had a half-formed attitude that they were too immature, yet in this mood he wondered if they might not be wiser than he was.

To his surprise, their tracks soon showed that they had turned off toward the old cabin instead of continuing on along the road that crossed directly over and dropped to the east side of the Piute. There wasn't anything wrong with that except that they had not come back this way, leaving him uncertain as to how to follow them. He decided to go on to the cabin, himself.

As he came out of the cedars into the little clear park he saw their horses at the ruins. Ty and Bernie were squatted about something on the ground that, from their actions, seemed to have them excited. Then they heard his horse coming and, to his surprise, they didn't look pleased to see him as he trotted on in. Then the thing at their feet registered, and a knife sliced coldly through him.

It was money, a heap of gold coins.

Zack felt his legs push against the stirrups, then he steadied and swung down.

"So this is the bank where you figured to get the money," he said in a grating voice. "Where did that pile come from?"

He knew he had caught them completely unawares, giving them no time to cover up, which they would surely have done otherwise. Ty stood with a slack face, while Bernie's eyes had turned cold and calculating. Behind them rose the ruins of the old fireplace Kelsey had built. They had been digging and prying around the stones of the hearth, he saw from the dirt-stained, splintered two-by-six they had been using. Some of the stones had been rolled out, and from under them had come this incredible pile of gold coins.

"So you decided to spy on us," Ty said bitterly.

"I didn't know you were here, but is that important? Maybe I'd better put my question different. What bank did it come from and when?"

Shrugging, Ty said, "Who knows? We didn't put it there. Kelsey did before he built that fireplace."

61

"Kelsey?" Zack thundered.

"Take a look at the mint dates. Not a one's less than twenty years old. We just finished counting it, and there's thirty thousand in that pile. Don't ask me where he got it. I don't know."

"How come you found it, then?"

"Just before we left here that night he told me there was money under the hearth but for us not to come back for it for a long, long time. You were busy with Evalyn, but I was where he could talk to me. I figured it was a hundred or so, the kind of money he'd get for his mustangs, and that he'd cached it there for a rainy day. It slipped my mind till Bernie and me were riding over the mountain. I told him, and we decided to take a look."

"How come I wasn't welcome here?" Zack countered. "You still didn't figure on telling me."

Ty's features blackened. "I wouldn't cheat you. I knew you'd say just what you did. That it was stolen."

"It was."

"You don't know that."

Zack ran his fingers through the tarnished discs, all of them eagles or better, and as Ty had stated the mint dates showed nothing of recent coinage. Looking into the hole from which the treasure had been removed he saw the remnants of a rotted gunnysack. It had been put there before the cabin was finished, all right.

"I'll be damned," Zack said, his breath shallow.

In a low, intent voice, Ty said, "Trying to figure out who to give it back to?"

"There was nothing in Kelsey's life to justify that much money, and you know it."

"He gambled when he was younger," Ty returned. "He said so."

"It belongs to somebody besides us."

"I knew you'd look at it that way," Ty said angrily. "So let me tell you something. Before I'll let you justify this country in what it done to Kelsey by making him look like a thief, I'll kill you. Is that clear?"

"Now, boys," Bernie cut in, "there's no need to go off half-cocked. This is a big surprise and it takes thinking about. Even if it wouldn't hang a dead man higher than a kite, Zack, there's no tracing where that money come from. Who'd know now—who could identify minted coins? The

62

amount wouldn't mean anything, either. Kelsey might have spent some or added to it. Whatever, you boys never knew a thing about it till just now. However he come by it, you're clean. And it sure would buy that herd and another half as big."

"I'm telling him," Ty repeated. "If he tries to turn it in he's dead."

Looking into his brother's eyes, Zack saw that he meant it. He shrugged.

Relenting a little, then, Ty said, "It's only money and that don't mean much to me. Maybe you won't believe it, but once in Leadville I had five thousand on the table in front of me. I could have taken it and been fixed for a long time, but I shot it on a bobtail flush. Money's only money, but I won't let Kelsey's name be drug in the mud again, and I mean what I said about that."

Smiling, Bernie said, "Yeah, it's a funny thing about that. I reckon just knowing it was there under his hearth made Kelsey feel safe all the time he lived here. It meant he'd never have to go back to grubbing out a living again. It meant he could stay here as long as he wanted. Take me, and that money would mean steers. Range. A spread so goddam big this country would tip its hat every time it looked my way. Thurm Quick never had nothing but me and trouble, which was about all he left me, too. You know what I'd like to do? Build me a great big house on that headland at the other end of this mountain where you can see the whole damned Piute. And I'd like to see my cattle running on every acre in sight. Not because it would make me a lot of money but because I'd be somebody. I'd get me a woman and have me a boy, and I'd sure make things different for him."

His eyes shining a little now, Ty said, "We're making a good start toward that."

Zack was still trying to figure it out. What the money meant was easier to determine than how it had got here. To Ty it meant excitement, perhaps the thrill of seeing it slip across a table into other hands. To Bernie it was power. To Kelsey it had been security, a guarantee against his return to the grubby world. Zack couldn't share that with Kelsey, for to him that had been cowardice. He couldn't share anything with Bernie or Ty other than his full awareness that reporting this find to the law would complete the defama-

63

tion of Kelsey's character and bring on a devastating showdown with Ty.

Roughly, he said, "I'll tell you what it means to me—plain rot. I want no part of it or of cattle or range bought with it, and if that's to be your intention, take notice. Bury that money again and forget it, or I'm on my way back to the prairies."

Ty's eyes widened. He hadn't expected that or even believed it could come.

Bernie put his hand on Zack's shoulder, but he looked at Ty. "I'll answer that. Zack's one of us like he's always been and I hope will always be. If that's the way he feels about it, we'll bury the dinero and forget we ever saw it. We'll borrow money for the steers and lease range, the way we planned."

Ty looked relieved, accepting that. Zack knew then that it really wasn't the money with him but his fear of letting the desert ranchers know how right they might have been in their judgment of Kelsey Maxon. Zack felt sick, knowing what he could not escape accepting about Kelsey. All he wanted was to bury the money as he had buried his wonder as to where Ty and Bernie had been when Loren Lee was killed.

9

Evalyn Trahan frowned slightly when she saw Ed Larkin ride up in front although she had been lonely during the three weeks since the Maxons left for the Malheur to bring in a new herd they had succeeded in buying for the new MQ. Passersby were usually poor company, and while Ed was considerably otherwise she felt sad sometimes when he was with her. That was because he *was* such a fine fellow and friend, and his cause was more hopeless now than it had ever been.

The only time he ever proposed marriage to her, she had explained very carefully to him, that she seemed to have been born in love with somebody else and that her feeling had never, could never change. Now that Ty was back, so attentive and admiring, not seeming to mind her being crippled at all, now that she was so happy, she wished that for his own sake Ed would stay away.

But when he came through the doorway Ed looked completely cheerful and matter-of-fact, and she eased. He was a man any fancy-free woman would find attractive. There was always a genial, half-amused expression on his lean, sandy features, and for all its slack length his body suggested a lithe power. She knew he was entirely fearless, yet it was the gentle quality of his nature that most appealed to her. Except for Ty Maxon she would have married him when he first came to the Piute.

He smiled and said, "Morning, Evalyn," as he came to the bar. He wouldn't want anything to drink this early and she stayed on the stool, knowing how pretty she looked there with the bad part of her cut from sight, and he stopped, opposite her. "On my way down to see Sam and wondered if there was any word you wanted to send Nancy."

Evalyn thought a moment. "I guess not, but thanks." His kindness was like that, mindful of the small things, and never forgetting.

"How's Mamma?"

"I think she's asleep," Evalyn answered. She had always been ashamed of her mother, of her grossness, her laziness and persistent need for attention. Her father had worn himself out on the old ranch, and Evalyn had never forgiven her mother for having been an utter burden and no help at all. Ed understood how demanding and petulant she was, but his unfailing kindness included her and was not feigned.

"Well, tell her I asked," Ed said, because he knew she would be offended if she learned he had been in and hadn't inquired about her. Then, as if in afterthought, he added, "By the way, the new herd just come in. Camped north of my place last night. They're holding there today while they cut it."

Evalyn knew that was why he had stopped in, to tell her without seeming to that Ty was back, and she felt a moving tenderness for Ed. But her voice was casual when she said, "They made good time."

"I guess them boys are real hands with cattle. I was at

65

their camp last night. They hired a road crew up north. They're going to keep it. Seems kind of queer. The Piute never had a big outfit before, and they're getting there fast."

"They got going in a hurry," Evalyn agreed.

She was immediately aware of the darkness that had moved across Ed's face. That surprised her for she knew it wasn't jealousy, of which Ed seemed to have none. She put it down to the natural suspicion aroused in a cattle country when some outfit began to grow and move swiftly. Range was range, and although rights existed strength could overcome them and often did.

Ed bought a sack of tobacco, a book of papers, paid for them and left. Afterward she didn't have to hide her happiness that Ty was back from Oregon. Already it seemed to her that the ten years separation had never happened, that their life together had been continuous and would go on unbroken.

In the kitchen Minnie Peebles was becoming noisy, and as she glanced at the wall clock Evalyn saw that it was nearly eleven, with barely an hour left before the northbound stage out of Piute and bound for Alta made its dinner stop. The same thing would be reversed in the evening when the southbound stopped for supper. Since the number of passengers who would want a meal could never be determined beforehand, Minnie had to be prepared to feed only a few or a multitude. A tall thin woman with a sharp nose and scanty straight hair, Minnie disliked uncertainties and right now would be mumbling to the potatoes about not knowing how many to peel.

Something clattered on the floor above, which Evalyn knew was Mamma's way of telling Minnie not to be so noisy, her room being directly over the kitchen. Minnie only got noisier; a state of war existed between the two women, Minnie silently fuming over the hulk of flesh up there and the three times a day she had to climb the stairs with a heaped tray so the lazy flesh could get fatter and lazier yet. Evalyn began to feel their chronic irritation flowing around her, nipping at her own nerves. Lafe Peebles, Minnie's husband, came in presently, washed and combed, and began to set the big table in the public dining room, a dozen places with the plates turned over to be used as required. He was a scrawny, discouraged

66

man, and he shared Minnie's steady complaint against life.

For the first time Evalyn let herself wonder what arrangements she would make if Ty asked her to marry him. Certainly she would not want to keep the tavern, but it was thriving and would be easy to sell. The problem was her mother, for she knew that next to marrying Ty the most alluring thing she could think of was getting a rest from her mother.

Then something happened that struck the bright mood from her. A horseman stopped and came into the bar, a young man with a hard face that lightened, even softened, when he saw her there on her stool. She saw the lift that came to him and was pleased, then it was all shattered when she reached up her crutches and swung onto them, for his face fell. Her spirits chuted with it, for she had seen that happen before, the undeniable demonstration of how many men felt toward her as she was now. He had a drink without a sociable word and went out.

When she dropped the coin he had left into the till, Evalyn's mouth twisted in faint bitterness. What made her think a man like Ty would want to make her his wife? She wasn't even sure she was capable of being a wife, of having children, even of giving a man the full pleasure of possession.

She was glad when the stage arrived with its balloon of dust. The driver came in and passed through to the kitchen to tell Minnie how many there were to feed. Watching through the window, Evalyn saw five, all men, stirring restlessly about the stage, staring here and there with complete indifference. Then they began to come in, three of them wanting drinks, one cigars. They took chairs in the bar, impatiently waiting for dinner to be served, expecting it to consist of the dreary fare of so many stage stations. She saw Peebles leading the team across to the barn, where it would be left, a fresh one going on with the stage. Then Peebles appeared from the kitchen, washed and combed again. Dinner was served, the passengers favorably surprised, and the stage went on. Two men in a wagon stopped after that to eat, then Peebles closed the dining room and took over the bar.

Evalyn went into her own downstairs room, which she had kept for convenience' sake even after the house became an inn, although she knew she should lift herself up

67

the stairs to visit with her mother a few minutes. Mamma would be minutely informed on everything that had happened outdoors, but after the driver and passengers had disappeared inside there would be a void she would want filled in. The stairs were a barrier—sometimes Evalyn considered it protective—between them. Mamma was so heavy on her feet she could not get up or down without having to stop to rest, puffing like a train, and that alone discouraged her from descending except for extraordinary reasons. Evalyn could make it up and down, but the stairs frightened her for once she had fallen from the middle landing and rolled and tumbled all the way to the bottom.

Alone in her room she let herself remember the man who had been deflated at seeing what she was really like. Lowering her weight onto the edge of the bed, she leaned the crutches against the side of the dresser and stretched out; her back was aching now, as it often began to do in the middle of the day.

The door opened, and Minnie looked in to say, "Don't you want your dinner?"

"I'll have something after a while, but don't bother to keep anything warm. It's just my back again."

Minnie nodded, not without sympathy, and closed the door.

Without meaning to do so, Evalyn found herself thinking of the night it all began, of her sick horror at the discovery that the men of the Piute, whom she had known all her life, meant to take Kelsey Maxon out and hang him. Kelsey had been such a kindly person, so easy for youngsters to know and get along with, maybe because he had never grown up completely himself. She remembered how she had waited in this very room until the sound of her mother's snoring told her her parents were asleep, appalled at the fact that they could think of sleep on a night that held so much terror.

Then she had got her pony and made that frantic ride. She recalled the awful hours up there, then their escape, and how she had nearly died while Ty and Zack were bringing her home, not because of her wound but because they had orders from their father to leave the Piute, and she knew they would obey since it was his wish. Then all the years since when she had never dared to hope they

68

would one day come back again—she had been dead through all of them.

She wondered as she lay in the day's mounting heat why she had been attracted to such wildlings as the Maxons. An obvious reason was the fact that Ty, Zack and Bernie were the only ones her age on the whole desert, but there had been more than that. She had felt alive with them and at the end, when she was in the change from child to woman, Ty had begun to make her feel as if she had been born just for him. There had been nothing that wasn't entirely innocent in the relationship; in fact she might have been more knowing than he, since her mother was always scolding and warning her. She had been dead for ten years, but now she felt alive again and —since that man with the disappointed eyes—hopeless.

She hated pity, and self-pity even more, and since she could not compel her mind to more cheerful thoughts, she shoved herself up with her arms, moved from there onto the crutches and slung out of the room. The Peebles were eating at the table in the kitchen, and she turned in there, unexpectedly wanting company. They were good people, simply turned shallow and irascible by the frictions of middle age.

"You eat now?" Minnie inquired.

"Just some coffee, Minnie."

"How about some peach pie?"

Minnie had baked these herself, her pride, so Evalyn said, "That sounds good." She took an empty chair and wondered why she always noticed how wet Peebles' mustache got from drinking coffee. At least he did not drink it out of his saucer as her father always had.

Minnie brought the coffee and pie. The tinkle of the bell over the barroom door announced that somebody had come in. Evalyn started to reach for her crutches, but Peebles said, "I'll get it," and went out.

Minnie said, "Your ma's mad at me again."

"What this time?"

"I forgot to take her tray up till she beat a hole in the floor."

Minnie hadn't forgotten, that was simply part of the warfare the two women carried on. Then Peebles came back and said, "Man wants to see you. One of them Maxons."

It never occurred to Evalyn that it might be Zack. She felt herself tremble as she reached for her crutches. She seemed to float onto them, then she was thumping out through the dining room and through the archway to the bar. Ty was on a stool with a drink Peebles had set up for him but came to his feet with a broad smile as she appeared.

"Hello, stranger," she said and blushed.

There wasn't a bit of the downcast look of the unknown man. Ty's eyes held their pleasure, and everything was all right again.

They sat at one of the tables in the barroom, and he told her about the drive. The Belkirk cattle were first-rate and it had been a lucky buy. There hadn't been any trouble although some of the going along the Owyhee desert had been hot and dry. The crossing of the region's streams posed no difficulty, and they had picked up good trail hands. There had been a branding chute at the Belkirk ranch, saving them a lot of time, and the cattle had trailed under the new MQ iron.

"Getting to be quite a brand," Evalyn said, excited.

"It's going to be bigger."

"Well, ambition doesn't hurt anybody. How's Zack?"

"The same old stick in the mud."

"Why, he's no such thing."

Ty smiled. "He's a real man, and I know it. He's in love with you, Evalyn. Do you realize that?"

The question startled her. "Well, I guess I wouldn't have called it being in love."

"So what's the ethics?" Ty said, furrowing his fine, high brow. "My brother wants you, so what do I do when I want you, too?"

He had said it.

"Lady's choice, Ty," she answered, putting her hand on his arm.

"Which does that mean?"

"I'm not ready to say."

But she was, ready to be crippled again for him, to die for him, to give him anything he asked.

10

The larger of the two cuts they had made up from the new herd that day was to go to the vegas east of Red Cedar to be grazed there until roundup. When the work was finished Zack rolled a cigarette with a look of satisfaction, Bernie noticed. Things were working out at a breath-taking pace and unbelievably well. The wire they sent from Piute had brought the reply that the herd had not yet changed hands. The price had been right, the cattle of surprisingly good quality.

Bernie had remained on MQ during the purchase and drive, and like Zack he sat on his heels now in the shade thrown by his horse. Ty had ridden down to see Evalyn as soon as the herd was cut. He and Bernie would go with the cattle moving to the east vegas, and Zack would take the rest home to be moved later onto the Garnet range acquired from Lee.

Tipping a nod toward the cattle, now being close-herded by the riders hired in the north, Bernie said, "That stuff's all too good to be shipped out for beef."

Agreeing, Zack said, "Too expensive to pasture it out all the time, though. We'd go broke."

"I know. We sure need more range of our own."

Bernie fell quiet when Zack gave him a quick glance. He was never entirely at ease with the redhead. Where he could read Ty readily because their minds and feelings ran the same, he always had an idea that Zack could read him while it didn't work the other way around. Not that this faint uneasiness had lessened his liking for Zack. They were both like brothers to him, the only ones he had ever had.

Ty had promised not to be gone too long for they had a few miles left to trail the cattle, and Bernie fell to speculating on the exact nature of Ty's interest in Evalyn. He wondered whether it was the real thing or if Ty was now worldly enough to know what he could have picked off back there, toward the last, and was now out to remedy the oversight. Bernie's mind drifted into a pleasant lewdness as it always did when he thought of women. Evalyn was all right for Ty, but he would take Nancy Milliron anytime, the fact that she was so disdainful of him only sharpening his interest. He had been around a lot since he reached manhood, probably knew more about women's hungers and weaknesses than Nancy did, and some day he might just give her a surprise.

Bernie had a persistent need for heady sensations. Too much dull routine made him restless as a caged animal, and he would thereafter need a big dose of excitement to throw it off. The restlessness was probably repressed energy, but it didn't feel like vitality so much as a growing deadness, with all death's fears mixed with it. When he had built up a charge like that he would usually hit the saddle, and once he had helped stick up a stage out of Bodie just to get the life back in him. He had been cooped up on MQ the last three weeks.

Ty was back promptly as promised. Afterward the cattle for the vegas were strung out. Bernie rode point with Ty for they would drop cattle at the ranches of George Castle, Newt Thursday and Frank Ashton, where they had made arrangements, and Bernie knew that part of the country better than Ty did. They made Castle's ranch the same night, cut out five hundred head and dropped them, leaving two men. On the second day they completed the delivery, and Bernie and Ty headed home through the gathering night.

It was the first time they had been alone since before the Maxons left for the north, and Bernie enjoyed it. He said, "Work's over, and it's time for some fun, ain't it?"

Laughing, Ty said, "What kind of fun?"

"Let's spend the night in town. I've been on that damned ranch ever since you left."

Ty simply swung his horse on a deeper slant to the south, which would take them around the end of Red Cedar to the north road before it struck out across the narrows. Before long, he said, "I'd like to take that pile of Kelsey's into the Big Chief and give those would-be high rollers a time."

72

"Get that out of your mind," Bernie advised. "Zack meant what he said about leaving it alone."

"He don't need to know everything."

"He don't," Bernie said and laughed. "But he's apt to take a look sometime to see if that dinero's still there or if we've dipped into it. And it better be there, or he'll head for the prairies like he threatened. What made him like he is and you like you are?"

"Our parents. It's the same as with calves, Bernie. Some draw from the bull's line, some from the cow's."

"Bulls in my line, I guess, and nothing else."

"You mean there's heifers on your mind and nothing else."

Bernie laughed.

They reached Piute around ten o'clock and their first stop was the Oasis Saloon, since they had eaten supper with Frank Ashton before leaving his ranch. The saloon held its usual boisterous crowd, mostly railroad hands, but they elbowed in to the bar.

Just before he lifted his shot of whisky, Bernie nudged Ty and said in a low voice, "Look who's down at the other end. And he's seen you. Looked like he'd swallowed a pail of lard. Old Ben Newkirk."

Ty's eyes gleamed as he studied the reflection in the back bar mirror. Newkirk quickly averted his glance. He fished into his pocket for a coin, dropped it on the bar top and slid back into the crowd.

Chuckling, Bernie said, "I bet he's scared stiff. He'll head for home, and it might be fun to be there when he arrives if he meant to stay here all night. He'll catch Jake in his shirt tail sure as hell. I've been waiting a long time for that to happen, and when it does Ben's going to beat you to Jake Michaels. The husband's always the last to know, but he likewise gets the most exercised when he finds out."

"Nobody's beating me to Michaels," Ty said.

"Likely Ben won't," Bernie agreed. "That affair's been going on for years, and Ben ain't smelled a rat yet. What he don't want he figures nobody wants, he's that stupid."

"He might not give a damn. Let Jake do the chores, and Ben can get his sleep."

They stepped back onto the street, but suddenly the many doors that opened from it had lost their excitement

73

for Bernie. Ordinarily he would have wanted at least to visit the Big Tent. The girls there were not supposed to conduct any private negotiations with the customers but some of them did. He knew one who would slip him the spare room key she carried as a favor to a few special frends. She was like Daycie in that she had a weakness for men and didn't want to spoil the fun of it by going professional. But Bernie suddenly had something even more interesting on his mind. He steered Ty out of the crowd drifting along the sidewalk and to the vacant bench in front of the watch maker's shop.

He said, "Set down a minute. Don't you think it's time MQ took on some more range so it can keep all the Belkirk cows?"

Ty gave him a hard stare. "You're sure busting your seams."

"Zack likes them new cows plenty. Said today it was a pity we can't keep 'em all for brood stock."

"Where's the new range?"

"Right now it's in the hands of Michaels and Newkirk."

"Hold your horses," Ty said sharply. "We've crowded our luck, already. If we bought more range and the men died, we'd swing. Where's your head?"

Bernie made an easy laugh. "Working for us. Nobody could object if we took a ranch or two off a poor widow woman's hands. That's how we got the new stuff."

"Daycie may be sleeping with both men, but she's only married to Ben."

"You want to bet it can't all be knocked down with one shake of the tree?" Bernie asked.

"Between now and shipping time?"

"Have to be before then to let us keep the cows."

Ty's interest was captured, as Bernie had known it would be. Ty said, "How much do you want to bet?"

"A hundred bucks?"

"You're on."

"Then the hell with this town," Bernie said. "Let's go home."

Daycie Newkirk was grumbling as she went half-heartedly about her morning's work. She was deeply affronted that Ben had taken it into his head to come home the night before after saying he would spend it in town

74

and catch up on his visiting. In consequence Jake had barely arrived and they were still in the kitchen having a drink of Ben's whisky when they heard Ben's horse and Jake had to clear out. If it had been two hours later, even an hour, she would not have had this unbearable feeling of unfulfillment. She didn't need whisky to want a man but when she had had it she wanted him twice as bad. She had even tried to stir Ben afterward but the old mummy had pushed her away and gone to sleep. She had laid there sleepless and half crazy all night.

There wasn't much in Daycie's life, never had been, except the one primitive happiness Ben interfered with or denied completely by his unexpected coming and going. She had been born over at the base of the Wasatch, one of several children of a woman who was one of several wives. You could tell somebody besides Daycie Newkirk that the plural marriages of the Mormons brought salvation—at least it hadn't for her. She doubted that she had even been missed when at thirteen she ran off, although that would be in part because she had never been very bright. She had been too stupid even to know what the man she had gone away with wanted of her, although when she found out she hadn't minded at all.

Men had been her one interest ever since. She never questioned whether what they gave her was love, she was important to them before and during the time they needed her, and even when they turned surly or mean afterward, she had the feeling of having been important to remember. Finally, some ten years ago, she had married Ben because she was tired of knocking about. He'd had a little power at first, but it soon left forever, and until Jake Michaels tumbled to what her eyes were saying to him there had been nothing for her but this rat-nest house and the desert.

She knew that even now in her early forties she was not a bad looking woman. Built big and roomy for having children, although for some reason she had never had any, she was nonetheless well shaped, although maybe too thin in the legs for the size of her rear and bosom. Her hair, which once had been yellow as corn in the ear, was now streaked with grey, and her skin had grown brown and coarse on the desert. But her eyes were pretty when something enlivened them, like a man or her memories of men.

They grew lively again when she heard a horseman coming on toward the house and saw, when she looked out, that it was not Ben coming back from the range but Bernie Quick. There was a man for you, although he had never once made a try for her.

She was holding her broom as she stood in the doorway watching Bernie ride up, and because of last night's frustrations she knew there was a certain light in her eye. Her heart made a thready little run when he touched his hat to her.

He said, "Morning, Daycie. Is Ben in the house?"

Daycie shook her head, and her chest was hollow when he promptly swung out of the saddle, dropped the reins and walked toward her, smiling. She thought she would faint when he spoke again, saying, "Well, it was you I wanted to see, anyway. How about a cup of coffee, Daycie?"

"Why, sure." Her breath was so short she could hardly speak. He had made all that hot ride to see her.

She tried to stand so he would brush her as he stepped on indoors. She was glad she had nearly finished cleaning up, although the place still wasn't much to look at. Bernie dropped his hat on the cluttered table, still smiling at her, stirring her unmercifully. He wouldn't, he couldn't have come here for the thing that kept streaking through her mind.

She told him to sit down and went into the kitchen to shake up the fire under the coffee pot. She and Ben drank it all day, always kept it ready. And it was good coffee. Back when she worked out it had always been as a cook. Which was the only thing about her Ben liked anymore, she thought with a grimace.

She took two cups of coffee in to the other room, and was pleased when Bernie took a taste and looked surprised that it wasn't the lye-like brew so typical of the cow country.

"That's all right," he said.

That made her very happy. "I never throw new grounds in with the old," she informed him. "I start fresh." Ben kicked about the extravagance of the habit, but it made her feel good to tell Bernie about it. She eyed him speculatively for his lack of hurry made her wonder if he hadn't had his thoughts on her a long while without her ever guessing.

76

As if understanding her curiosity, Bernie said, "What you going to do, Daycie, if something catches up with Ben like it did with Loren Lee?"

Coffee sloshed and ran down the side of Daycie's cup. She didn't give a hoot about Ben. It was Jake she was worried about. He was as deep in the muck as Ben in connection with that old Maxon case. She knew what she'd do in a minute if Ben alone got it, she'd marry Jake.

"You think them Maxon boys killed Lee?" she asked. "It was in the paper that the sheriff thinks horse thieves done it."

"What does Ben think?"

"He tried to believe what the sheriff said. But when he come home last night after seein' Ty Maxon in town, he was scared out of his wits. That pair's staying at your place. You think they done it?"

"All I know," Bernie said, "is that they had a good reason. But they're friends of mine, and I ain't accusing 'em, Daycie. But Lee was a bachelor and Ben's married, and I've been kind of worried for your sake. This ranch'd be yours, and it's more'n a woman could handle."

Daycie stared at him with an open mouth. It was true that the ranch would come to her; she had never thought that far ahead. The thrilling thought came into her mind: And I could marry Jake, and no more having to keep an eye out for old Lord Limber. She wondered if the Maxons would kill Ben; then, if they were going to, why they didn't hurry and get it done. Suddenly there was nothing she had wanted so bad in her whole life.

"What'd you do, Daycie?" Bernie pressed.

"Jake'd marry me in a minute." Daycie looked startled. She hadn't meant for that to pop out. That was the trouble with her head, it never worked as fast as her tongue. But Bernie didn't look shocked.

"That's be the sensible thing," Bernie agreed, nodding his head. "That'd give him a fine big ranch and a real pretty wife."

"You think they'll do it?" Daycie said eagerly.

Bernie laughed. "Even if I knew, I wouldn't say, Daycie. They're friends of mine."

He rose suddenly, leaving her with such a stirring new excitement that she didn't think to wonder why he had come, for he hadn't said much, actually.

77

"Thanks for the coffee," he said and walked out.

When she heard his horse leave she tossed out the cold coffee in her cup, went into the kitchen to pour more. Then she sat down at the table there, her eyes glowing with this strange, unexpected excitement. A new idea was stirring with it. Jake hated Ben, particularly since the Maxons had come back. Only last night he had been grumping about it being Ben who got them started after Kelsey Maxon that night by reporting that he had been on a trip north, the same direction in which Jake had trailed the horses he'd had stolen.

A wild impatience filled Daycie as she thought that out. The Maxons had dallied a whole month since killing Lee, might wait another if they ever killed Ben, while she could not wait another day. She knew Ben's habits well. He had left about an hour ago. First he would go to Hunsaker Well to see if there were any steers to be pulled out of the bog. From there he would ride up into the Garnets where the summer cattle were, coming back farther north for a stop at Indian Spring, then home, which he wouldn't reach until supper time. She had most of the day. Jake never showed up here by daylight, nor would he let her come to his place, but this time she was going over to see him.

She was riding out within minutes after this decision, forking the saddle and not caring any more than she ever did that her dress hiked up to show a considerable length of bare leg. None of Ben's horses were any good and the one he let her use was windbroken and incapable of more than a jarring trot. The sun came down mercilessly on her bare head, but she thought she could intercept Jake about this time of day at his waterhole at Magnetic Hill. There were cedars there, and it would be pleasant and private. She rode with the stoic patience of a squaw.

She reached the hill ahead of him, rode in among the trees and slid down from the horse. Trailing the reins, she left the beast and moved to the outermost tree, where she seated herself in the shade, able to see the waterhole and its collected steers below her. Jake would be angry about her recklessness but after last night's disappointment he would soon forget, and then she would tell him what was in her mind. She was there nearly an hour, but it was pleasant sitting in the shade and thinking of the future

78

that had suddenly opened before her. Then she saw Jake riding down from the Garnets, breaking out of a canyon across from her and coming forward. Her heart began to race.

He rode warily, watching his surroundings as if he expected something to happen at any moment, and thus she was able to attract his attention, when his glance lifted up the knoll, and save riding down into the heat. It took a moment for him to reassure himself about who she was, then he spurred his horse.

He was scowling furiously as he rode up. "What the devil are you doing here, Daycie?" he demanded. "You trying to get us into trouble?"

She waggled her fingers at him. "I can't hear what you say way up there."

Jake swung out of the saddle, still uneasy and angry, and the way his muscular legs knotted against his shrunken pants made her breath catch. He didn't come on down to her as she had invited him but his staring eyes began to take on that funny light she knew, so ready and over-riding, and she knew he couldn't stay mad much longer, at least until after he had taken advantage of the opportunity she had created.

Grinning suddenly, he said, "I always wondered how it'd be in daylight. You still don't look bad."

That was about as close to a compliment as he had ever come. Smiling up at him, Daycie said, "Pretty soon it won't have to be the barn, Jake. We can live like married folks."

Jake had started to lower himself beside her, but he shot upright. "Married folks? Has something happened to Ben?"

"Well, now, it could," Daycie teased.

She saw the blood run out of his ruddy cheeks. "The Maxons! They warned him?"

"Well, they might."

"Daycie!" Jake thundered. "What are you driving at?"

"You know something, Jake?" Daycie said dreamily. "If they kill Ben the spread's mine. You ever think of that? You wouldn't be getting a poor woman. That spread's better than yours, too."

"If they kill Ben, I'll be next, even if I ain't first. You're talking crazy, woman." He sat down beside her and began

79

to rub his bearded face, excited suddenly. It wasn't fear, all at once, and she knew it wasn't because she was here and ready for him. A smile built on the heavy lips of his wet mouth as he stared out across the little hill-locked valley. "Maybe not. Maybe you ain't, at that."

Daycie waited because it had to be his idea.

"By damn, Daycie," he said presently, "Ben and me're both set up, and maybe I'm smart enough to beat 'em. Maybe that woolheaded sheriff needs showing he should have listened to what I told him. Them five shots Lee took—" Jake's heavy voice trailed off, and again he was thinking earnestly.

"What about them five shots?" Daycie prodded.

"If Ben wound up with five slugs in him, that sheriff would stop talking about horse thieves. Wouldn't he? Wouldn't it show the killers was still on the Piute, men who hated both Lee and Ben?"

"I don't guess I know what you mean, Jake."

Patiently, he explained, "It'd prove the Maxon boys done it. A man empties his gun into somebody only when he hates him like hell. That's why some took it to mean the Maxons killed Lee. If it happened again, they'd be up the creek, with even the sheriff convinced. Daycie, that's all it takes to keep 'em from getting around to me."

"Maybe they wouldn't do it that way again," Daycie worried.

"Maybe not. But what if somebody else done it?"

Now he was getting the idea that had brought her here. "Like you?" she encouraged.

He looked at her, shocked. "Like you."

"Oh, Jake—no!"

"Ain't the old boy cheated you out of your rights ever since you been married to him? And what're you going to do for a man who can handle you if the Maxons get me? Don't fool yourself, Daycie. You ain't no competition for the young girls, no more."

Daycie was as horrified by his suggestion as he had been by hers. Born of her urgency to have it happen, there had been in her mind the idea that to get her and Ben's ranch, Jake would do it and let the Maxons be blamed for it, saving her from uncertainty and waiting, but that was as far as she had thought it out. If he threatened not to see her again unless she did it, she knew she would succumb.

80

He was right about her not attracting men as she once had. Bernie Quick could have had her for the asking that morning, and the thought never entered his head.

"Oh, Jake," she moaned.

"You want them to kill me, too?"

"Oh, no!" she cried.

"They've got their sights on me, I'm telling you. Help me out, and they'll be hung. We'll have us a fine big ranch and nobody to come busting in on us in the middle of things."

"I'd be too scared."

"Where's the danger? Pump five shots into the old boy and it'd be like the Maxons had signed their names on his carcass."

"You'd marry me then?"

"Any time you say."

The desire that had ridden her since the night before had been scared out of Daycie, and Jake seemed to have forgotten his own. In a way it was sweet, just sitting here thinking of their being able to act like any married couple.

Finally she said, "All right, but you've got to marry me right away afterward. No stalling, or I'll tell the sheriff who done it and who put me up to it." Daycie had had experience with men's promises. She wasn't going out on a limb without some kind of a surety bond.

"The minute you're a widow," he promised. "Now, you be careful about it. Don't leave any sign to tie you in, or you won't be in shape to get married."

Daycie remembered something that had happened in a town where she once worked. "Somebody come to the door," she imagined. "Middle of the night. Old Lord Limber went to the door and got pumped full of lead. That woke me up, and I heard horses leaving."

"You looked out the window," Jake improved, "and saw it was a couple of fellows. It struck you it was the Maxons. Don't say it was them, because you couldn't be sure in the dark. Just say you got that impression. You'll have to use Ben's gun, and be sure and clean it good afterward. Then go to Trahan's for help, not here. Don't you get me mixed up in it, Daycie."

"I won't."

She was trying to steel herself to it, but she wished he

81

would kiss her and tell her just once that he really loved her.

"Just remember. I ain't coming to see you till it's done."

Fear shook her, and she cried, "Make love to me, Jake. It's all right here."

He laughed and rose to his feet. She knew she would never have him again until she had done what he said. She was so frightened she was sick, for this was not at all what she had come here for.

11

Zack left MQ with a wagon around eight, that morning. Bernie had already saddled a horse and ridden off somewhere, as he did so unpredictably, but sometime that day he and Ty were to move the new cattle into the Garnets to be run there until fall roundup. Mainly, Zack wanted a load of stock salt from Piute, since the steers had grown hungry for it on the trail, and Bernie had only a small supply. Also, the food vanished rapidly now that there were three men living on the ranch, and they had worked up a large grocery order the night before. He wanted to make the round trip that day, although it would take him well into the night.

Seated on the sheepskin padding of the wagon seat, he took stock, as he usually did, of the morning. The sun's slanting rays were already heating the desert fearfully so that the air wavered all about him, and distant objects were distorted like reflections on the surface of disturbed water. The colors stood out on the rocks where the light struck fully or they changed into vague, dark smears where shadow overlay them.

It did not take long to reach the Alta trail, which he crossed although he could have followed it to the junction. It was only neighborly that he stop at Milliron's to see if there was anything he could bring from town, and the extra distance was trivial. Sam had tried to set a decent basis for the future. He wanted to show that he was of a like mind, although it was probable that Ty would always hate the big, cleft-chinned man he had killed symbolically so long ago on the cattle trail to Wyoming.

The going across the open range was rough, but there were only two or three miles of it, and he traveled steadily by following the ruts left by roundup wagons over the years. He cut the north road just at the Milliron headquarters and drove up the short lane to the house. By the time he got there, curiosity had drawn Nancy to the front porch.

Smiling, Zack lifted a hand to his hat and said, "Morning, Nancy. I wondered if you need anything I can bring from Piute."

She looked pretty in her house dress with her hair braided and wrapped around her head. Her skin had a fine color, tanned but not enough to submerge a nice pinkness in her cheeks. She surprised him by not showing the faint uneasiness he had sensed in her when he was here before. Possibly it was his courtesy that had made the change, or perhaps her father had persuaded her that he meant no harm.

She said, "Why, I was driving the buckboard in today, myself."

"No need if it's something I could bring."

Ruefully, she said, "We're out of flour, and you'll probably have enough of a load." Then all at once she smiled. "The truth is, I want something to do today."

He surprised himself when he said promptly, "I'll be late getting back, but you're welcome to come along with me. It's a lonesome trip when a person makes it by themselves."

"I know it is. You'd better mean that invitation. I've got a good mind to take you up."

"Come on," he said and did mean it.

It took a while for her to get ready, but he didn't mind waiting. When she emerged from the house again she wore a slimly tailored skirt with narrow blue and white stripes, a white shirtwaist and a straw sailor hat. His mouth opened in frank admiration, but that get-up wasn't sensible in all the dust. Yet he had learned not to advise a woman on matters of her dress, and he said nothing as he reached down to help her up to the seat with him.

"Dad's out somewhere," she said, "but I left a note that

I'll be late. This is a bother for you. Maybe you intended to get drunk in town."

"If I do you can drive home."

She laughed with him and he was sure that, whatever had reassured her, she was ready to be friends.

A breeze sprang up as they turned south on the main road, rolling the dust off to the right so that it no longer boiled up around the wagon, and Zack was especially pleased by this unexpected development. Off to the east the long, purple mass of Red Cedar ran into the dissolving forward distance. Nancy grew so quiet he thought she had turned shy with him again, but when he stole a glance he saw a relaxed face. She was simply enjoying the morning and the slow progress of the ride. A person could take his time and see things from a wagon seat that he missed when kiting along on a horse.

Finally Nancy broke her silence, saying, "Did the Belkirk cattle live up to promise?"

"More than did. I aim to thank your dad for the tip."

Impulsively, she burst out, "Zack, I'm glad you don't bear a grudge against us. I was such a lonely kid. I think I would have liked you back then." That told him why she had changed toward him since the last time. Sam or her own judgment had convinced her.

"Saplings bend the way of the trees around them," Zack reflected. "At least that's what I heard an old Indian say. I thought you were a scrawny, snooty brat."

"Scrawny, indeed, but not snooty. Just scared of such wild boys. Why don't people trouble to learn the truth about each other?"

"Harder proposition than just taking the trouble."

"I know," she agreed. "Like Dad. He bends over backwards now to be fair. That awful thing changed your life, Zack, and if it's any comfort it changed his and mine, too. He's gone through hell."

The end of Red Cedar slipped into the distance behind; ahead loomed the desert narrows between Smoke Tree and Red Rock, the furnace stretch of the trip to town. Away from the draughts created by the mountain the air grew dead, scorching and still. Fortunately, the sterile, sandy earth rolled up less dust or they would have smothered.

"Did you know that some of the emigrants crossed here going into Oregon from the Humboldt?" Nancy asked.

"Dad used to talk about them. Before they learned the best route, it must have been dreadful. When he first came here there were skulls all along the old wagon tracks. There was no water for the oxen, no grass, and at first they took the worst part of the desert."

"They were hardy people. Compared to them we're soft and pampered."

She laughed. "That takes a stretch of the imagination, but I guess we are."

As they moved farther onto the narrows the air grew hotter. Looking down at Nancy, Zack saw how the heat had brought up a dew that curled the loose hair at her forehead. But she had known that the wagon would be slow and didn't seem to mind it.

Then, as if divining his concern, she said, "You're worrying about my comfort, so I'd better confess. I had no intention of coming to town today. I got myself invited so I could get acquainted with you. Do you know that no young man has ever taken me anywhere before? There just aren't any."

"What's the matter with Bernie's eyesight?"

"He's your partner and an old friend but—well, we just don't see eye to eye on things."

"There's Ed Larkin."

"He's never seen anybody but Evalyn."

Zack frowned at that reminder, for Bernie had mentioned the same thing. He liked Larkin's appearance, expected to get along with him. But he also liked Evalyn, and if there was any chance she could care for anyone but Ty, he aimed to try his hand.

"So I don't know how to act," Nancy was saying, "and I suppose I'm too forward."

"Honest women don't come along any oftener than honest men. I like them."

"Thank goodness. Tell me about your life after you left here."

So he talked about that, the trail, the winter in Deadwood, then his years with the Union Cattle Company. "Big outfits like that are mighty interesting," he commented. "The set-up's different to the way an independent operator works. The main difference is that the big companies have the money it takes. We had five different ranches, one on the South Platte, another in the sandhills, one near Lusk, and one west of the Black Hills. Eventually there was one in the Laramie Basin, as well."

"Why so spread out?"

"The different ranches did different things," Zack explained. "At first the one on the South Platte received cattle from Texas. Later, when everything came from Oregon and Idaho, the one in Laramie Basin took over that job. The others were cow and calf ranches, while the ones closest to the railroad were for steers. The stuff went through the works like hay through a bailer, thousands of head moving all the time, maybe a hundred thousand on the range. They had a feed lot down close to Omaha. I worked down there a couple of times. The biggest barn held four thousand head doing nothing but eat and get fat. The regular hands would winter down there then go back to the range in the spring."

"You liked it, didn't you?" Nancy observed. "Then why did you come back to the Piute?"

"Ty wanted to come out here somewhere."

"You're awfully close, aren't you?"

He glanced at her quickly. "We're brothers."

She fell silent, and he supposed she was still doubtful of Ty, who had made no effort to be friendly. As a matter of fact, he admitted he was doubtful himself as to what the relationship would be between Ty and Sam Milliron as time went by.

They reached Piute just before two o'clock. "Now, don't you worry about me," Nancy said as they stopped at the wagon yard. "I'll find lots of things to do. Just look me up when you're ready to leave."

"I was thinking about dinner," Zack said. "I'm hungry, and since you're an honest woman, I hoped you'd admit you're empty."

"I could eat a raw cow."

"You can get it from bellering to burnt in this town. Wait and we'll go to the hotel dining room."

"If it won't make you sorry you got me on your hands."

They had a good dinner at the Nevada, then Nancy vanished into a store. Going to the feed dealer's, Zack ran into trouble. "I ain't got a bit of salt," the man said. "Either I'm loaded to the eaves with something nobody wants or everybody's after the same thing. Lately it's been

86

salt, but there ought to be some in on the freight this afternoon. It was due yesterday."

"When's the freight?"

"Around eight this evening. The salt's been shipped. I wired to find out."

Zack left his orders, and went out on the street, thinking that if he had been alone he would wait, but it wouldn't do to keep Nancy away from home that late. So he would have to go back and come in again in another day or two. He found her in the dress goods department of the store she had entered and told her.

"Why, you won't make two trips because of me," she returned. "That would make me feel just fine for foisting myself on you. We'll wait for that freight train."

"Won't your father worry?"

"I told him I'd be late."

"But not that late."

"I told him I was coming in with you."

Zack wondered how reassuring that would be to Sam Milliron. But Nancy was insistent, nor would she listen to his suggestion of getting her a horse at the livery so she could return whenever she wanted. He went over to the grocery department and placed the big order he had brought with him, arranging to pick it up at the wagon platform in the rear of the building. By the time he had finished, Nancy had left the place. The wall clock above the shelves of tin cans told him he still had four hours to kill before the evening freight came in from the east.

All the way to town with Nancy he had been conscious of his shaggy hair, which had not been trimmed since he left Cheyenne, so he went to a barber shop. The place was crowded, and he killed nearly an hour before he emerged, feeling much better. He saw nothing of Nancy on the street but decided against going to a saloon for a drink as long as she was along with him. He wound up in a chair on the hotel porch, that haven of the unoccupied.

He loaded the groceries at six o'clock, left the wagon tied on the street, then found Nancy in his old chair on the hotel porch. By the time they had finished supper in the dining room, the freight came in and the salt came with it. In the gathering night they started home. The prospect was not at all unpleasant, for it would be much cooler crossing the narrows.

87

"Well, you got your day killed," Zack commented.

"It's been very nice. And your haircut's nice, too."

He was pleased that she had noticed, then decided she couldn't help it after the crop of wool he had been wearing. They hit it off remarkably well; from the start he had been at ease with her, feeling no need to talk unless he wanted, not worried about her own long silences. Her mind was quick, trenchant, and he decided that she must have read a great deal in addition to the barely adequate country school training they all got. It was odd that the desert could have produced her, for she couldn't have known anything else. Yet he knew its capacity for creating rare beauty as well as raw ugliness.

The night deepened, the stars emerged, and it grew cooler. The loaded wagon pulled harder, yet rode easier than it did when it was empty. Its rumble was a low melody against the night's scattered sounds. He began to feel a peace he had not known since he had left Red Cedar. For the first time he was truly glad he had come back, and he realized there had been a trace of nostalgia in him when he told Nancy about his years with Union.

Kelsey had been wrong in sending them away, for a man could not find himself except in the place where he first became lost. It would work for Ty too; it had to take that churning restlessness, that drive for some obscure attainment, out of him.

"When I was a little girl," Nancy said abruptly, "I used to think of these deserts as a moat between us and the scary world. Kind of a hot moat, wasn't it? I liked to feel protected and safe, then I got to hating it. Why is it that the world both scares and draws you so strongly?"

"You want to see the big wide world?"

"Yes and no. I'd like to know what it is I expect to find out there."

"You wouldn't find it," Zack said, "but I know what you mean. You want the emptiness in you filled up, that's all. The thing that will do it is as apt to come to you on the Piute as it is to be found off somewhere."

"You do know what I mean," she mused. "I'm so empty, Zack. Why?"

"If I could answer that I could answer the biggest question in the world. But I can tell you this. You'll know it if it ever comes along."

88

She fell back into her silence; the wagon rolled on through the night.

They were coming off the narrows, somewhere near midnight, when far ahead a horseman emerged in the starlight, riding toward them fast. The shape enlarged, and in a few minutes Nancy let out a cry.

"That's Peebles—Evalyn's hired man! Something must be wrong there!"

Zack had seen Peebles at Trahan's roadhouse and recognized him as he came nearer. The man identified the occupants of the wagon and pulled up when he came abreast.

"What's wrong?" Nancy asked sharply.

"Another killing," Peebles said in a tight voice. "I'm going for the sheriff."

"Killing?" The word was Zack's, low and hollow. "Who?"

"Ben Newkirk. Somebody pumped him full of lead in his own doorway. Five shots again. His woman came to Trahan's. She said there was two of 'em." Peebles stared at Zack in sudden bewilderment. "By damn, she said she thought one was you and the other your brother."

"Oh, no," Nancy moaned.

"Well, it sure couldn't have been him," Peebles said, tipping his head at Zack. "And I better get riding again."

"What time was it?" Zack asked.

"She said soon after dark." The man went on.

"It's happened again," Nancy said in a hoarse whisper. His voice was rough. "Maybe if you hadn't been with me all day, you'd think it was me and Ty too."

"Not you," she said weakly, "but I've got to say it, Zack. How about Bernie and—and Ty?"

Anger boiled in him, but he couldn't answer that when, deep inside, the same question squirmed in himself.

He drove on in dazed silence, aware mostly of the crushed, frightened girl beside him. He didn't blame her a bit. Two of the four men who had killed Kelsey Maxon were now dead, both killed since the return of Kelsey's sons, and her father was one of the two men left alive.

12

When Ty heard the rumble of the wagon, he looked across the table at Bernie and said with relief, "Here he comes, finally. Must have dished a wheel on the narrows or something." They had been playing poker without much excitement because they were using beans, and both dropped their card hands and shoved up. They were in the yard waiting when Zack drove in with the loaded wagon.

"So you made it," Ty said. "I was beginning to wonder if somebody waylaid you."

He got a shock when he saw Zack's face, but Zack came down over the front wheel before he answered. It looked like he really had had that kind of trouble.

"Nobody waylaid me," Zack said, "but I just heard somebody fixed Ben Newkirk. Dropped him in his doorway. Five shots again, and his wife said there were two men again. She also said they looked like the Maxon boys."

"Is this a joke?" Ty said, disbelieving.

"If it is, Peebles is going to catch hell from the sheriff. He's heading for Piute to wire, and we met him this side of the narrows. Ben's wife came to the roadhouse. She said it happened right after dark."

Ty couldn't accept it or help throwing a bleak, protesting look at Bernie. But Bernie himself looked stunned. Ty could feel Zack's cold gaze rake his features.

"Who could have done it?" Ty gasped.

"The sheriff will really want to know, this time."

"How could Daycie say she thought it was you boys?" Bernie put in with a hollow voice. "Hell, that upsets it, right there. Zack was in town. A lot of people seen him there."

"Moreover," Zack said, "I had company both ways. Nancy Milliron rode in with me and back. But that still doesn't prove there wasn't a Maxon involved."

"Kid, are you trying to say—?" Ty began in a deadly voice.

"I'm only saying what the sheriff will think. Lee and Newkirk down, both pumped full of lead by two men. Michaels and Milliron to go. He's going to want to lock somebody up quick, and everybody else will want him to."

His voice strained with false cheer, Bernie said, "We won't take off our boots till we come to the river. We kept your supper warm, Zack. We'll put up the team. You go in and eat."

"We ate in town. The store was out of salt, and I had to wait for the late freight."

"Go get a cup of coffee, anyhow."

Without answering, Zack walked across the porch and into the house. Springing up to the seat, Bernie drove the wagon on to the barn. Ty walked behind, then helped unhitch, water the horses and turn them out.

At the pasture gate he said bitterly, "So you shook the tree and it all come down. I suppose you're ready to collect that hundred dollar bet we made."

Bernie sent a nervous glance toward the house, but they were too far off for Zack to overhear them. Desperately, he said, "So help me, I don't know what happened. I went to see Daycie this morning, all right. It was a gamble, that's all. To put the idea in her fuzzy head of what she'd gain if old Ben was knocked off. I figured when it didn't happen, she'd make it happen and make Jake marry her. Don't you see the play? If she was widowed again, after marrying Jake, she'd have to sell out. She couldn't run one spread, let alone both. It'd be a safe buy for us. I was out to win that bet, all right, and I'd like to know who horned in."

"Nobody did. She killed Ben, all right. And pumped five shots into him and told that yarn about us to frame us for it."

Bernie snorted. "Daycie ain't that smart. Cunning enough to put wolf poison in Ben's coffee or something like that. At his age, nobody'd think twice if he just up and died. She wouldn't have to frame you, and anyway she ain't smart enough to figure all that out."

Ty had started a cigarette, but his hands shook so he couldn't finish rolling it. Dropping the crumpled paper, he

91

said, "This way she protects Jake, too. She figures that if we go to jail we won't be able to get at him."

"Jake!" Bernie said in an all-gone voice. "He seen a way to save his own hide. He did it or put her up to it."

"Clever as hell, aren't you?" Ty said savagely.

"You've got to get an alibi."

"Where?"

After a moment, Bernie said, "Evalyn."

"You're crazy."

"So's she—about you. She already knows the fix you're in. She'll say you were there."

"Damn you, Bernie, you've made things bad enough. I won't drag her into it."

Softly, Bernie said, "Rather hang because Jake Michaels framed you? Remember, two men again, the same as laid for Lee. Five shots again, and this time somebody has pointed a finger straight at you. Not at me. I didn't have the reason to hate Ben you had. I don't need an alibi, you do. Zack's got one. If you got one, it would knock Daycie's story into a cocked hat. Go over and see Evalyn."

Ty took a turn around in a nervous circle. He had never been this frightened before. Doing something and expecting to have to pay for it if you got caught was one thing, a kind of wild excitement he liked. But getting caught innocently in a web of circumstantial evidence was something else. He had a feeling of being overwhelmed, crushed. His wits were no good to him now, for the thing had simply exploded in his face without warning.

But he was glad Zack was out of it, he had never deceived himself that his brother wasn't ten times the man he was. He tried desperately and uselessly to find a way to extricate himself. There was only way, and Bernie had mentioned it—Evalyn. No one else on the Piute would care to help him, and she would any way she could. It all depended on whether the situation at the tavern would permit her to say he had been there at the time Daycie said Ben was shot down. He could at least find that out.

"I've got to talk to her," he said finally.

Bernie's sleek mind was working fast. He said, "Just remember it's Jake Michaels trying to frame you—the man who fired the shot that killed Kelsey. The man who says even today it was good riddance."

"Tell Zack I was afraid she'd been upset and went over to see her."

Ty was soon riding out, hating himself for what he had in mind. But the inevitability of it grew more and more apparent as he headed across the range. His hatred of Jake Michaels burned at twice its former intensity. He was positive that after the idea was planted by Bernie, Daycie had discussed killing Ben with Jake, who had seen how to turn it against the men he feared. Michaels would now pay for that as well as for Kelsey, Ty swore, no matter what the outcome would be for himself.

He knew it was around two o'clock in the morning by now. The roadhouse would be shut up, and he would have to tap on Evalyn's window and awaken her. But he had to talk to her before she saw the sheriff or it would be too late. He stopped his horse at the edge of the trees beside the house and swung down, his legs trembling. For a moment he nearly backed out, then forced himself forward.

He slipped in easily to the side of the tavern by her window, whose ground-floor location he remembered well. Several times when they were younger, and Evalyn as athletic as any boy, she had slipped out to join them in some night adventure. His mind went back yearningly to that carefree time: no troubles, no ambitions beyond those of the lazily passing days. Why, in the end, had Kelsey thought that so bad for them? Ever since, Ty had tried to recapture the feeling; not once, since he left here, had he had it for a moment.

He made the old scratching sound on the window glass. If she heard it and remembered, it would bring her promptly. He waited through several breaths then saw the shape of her through the dark glass, the white of her nightgown. She stared out curiously, then recognized him. The sashes, which she had lowered from the top for protection, lifted upward under her tugging hands.

Her frightened voice whispered, "Ty—what is it?"

"I've got to talk to you, so I guess I'll have to come in."

She looked around nervously, then nodded her consent.

He lifted himself up, moved silently through and stood facing her in her bedroom. The light held by the night showed him she was on her crutches, her hair in braids, her face drawn with the fear he had evoked, perhaps the fear that he was guilty.

"I didn't do it," he whispered. "You know that, don't you?"

"Oh, yes," she whispered back, almost too vehemently.

"But it's the second time a man's been killed, and the second time I can't prove I didn't do it, Evalyn. Zack went to town and was late getting back, and Bernie and me stayed at the ranch waiting for him. It's the same as when Lee was killed. We can say we were home but there's nobody to back it."

"I'm sorry," she said.

As yet she hadn't seen what he wanted of her. But she would if he kept nudging her mind. "I wanted to come over here for the evening," he said regretfully, "and it's sure too bad I didn't. There must have been people here who could say they saw me."

"Probably. I came to bed at ten o'clock. It was my back again."

Urgently, he said, "Did you go out when Daycie Newkirk came?"

She shook her head. "Minnie called through the door, and I told her to send Peebles to Piute to wire the sheriff. Daycie wouldn't stay."

Frustration swelled in him. If Evalyn had come to bed early, didn't even know who had been in the tavern that evening, there was no chance of finding a way she could help clear him. She swung herself quietly to the bed, sat down and stood her crutches against the dresser. He saw her shiver.

"Better lie down and cover up," he whispered. "I'll go in a minute."

"Don't go."

But she swung her legs up onto the bed, and pulled a blanket over her lower body. He sat down on the bed's edge, watching her. Strange as it was, considering his fear, she was a stirring sight there, so intimately appealing. He knew there was little chance of their being surprised here at this hour for since the house had been remodeled hers was the only downstairs bedroom and their whispering would not carry to any listening ears.

He didn't tell her about Bernie's visit to Daycie Newkirk. He said that they suspected Michaels of trying to frame him and Zack, out of his magnified fear for his own life. That was what made it such a bitter pill, considering

94

what Michaels had helped do to him, and to her as well. She agreed. She kept pressing the heel of her hand to her forehead, trying to think.

"I wish I'd questioned Daycie," she moaned. "I might have tangled her up, and maybe the sheriff can, if he gets on the right track. She's a slut and hardly more than an idiot, but after the Lee case her story will have weight if it isn't knocked to pieces. If only you'd gone to town with Zack."

"Or come here," he reminded her. "Well, I didn't, and if it looks too bad I can always clear out."

"Oh, Ty—no! You've just come back!"

"It might be that or hanging."

She was crying quietly. Suddenly he bent forward, slid his hands behind her thinly covered shoulders and lifted her toward him. Her palms came up to cup his face, and they kissed for the first time in all the years they had spent together. She stayed thus for a long time, then fell back, sighing.

"You *were* here," she whispered. "In my room all night. That's why I came to bed early. The Peebleses never come in here, and Mamma hasn't been downstairs in a week. That's it, Ty. It's got to be the story."

"You can't say a thing like that! And if you think I would—!"

"You couldn't. But maybe I wouldn't have to tell anyone but Webster. He likes me, and it would force him to work on Daycie, and that might clear the whole thing up."

"And it might not," he returned. "Somebody's proved himself pretty foxy over there."

"Then I'll testify in court."

"Do you think I'd let you do a thing like that? Helping save me from a frame-up is one thing. Ruining your reputation's another."

"What good's my reputation if you go away again?"

"I won't let you. I'm riding, right now."

"No!"

Her hands caught him and pulled him down. Her mouth hunted his in desperate seeking. He felt the lifting beat of his heart, heard its pulse crash in his ears, and still she smothered him with her fear and her yearning.

"I wish you had been here," she whispered. "Even without the trouble. Stay with me till morning."

95

"Evalyn—!"

She would not accept his refusal.

Later, when he lay beside her, he was no longer frightened. He had hoped that her love would save him, he had been amazed at its depth, at her joy in giving herself to him. With a wrench of the heart he thought of the night when she had been crippled for him, for he had known it was for him mainly that she came up to Red Cedar. When he told her goodbye, before he went away with Zack, there had been a look on her face he had seen just now in the starlight.

She wouldn't let him go until they could see the morning star through her window. When finally he rose and began to dress, he said, "I won't go away. I know what the truth is. I'll stand on that, whatever comes."

"I know what it is, too. You're innocent, and I love you."

"And I love you, too." When he had pulled on his boots, he came to a stand. Looking down, he added gently, "There've been women, but never one like you. There never will be one like you."

"I'm glad."

"But don't you say anything to Webster about this—do you hear me?"

She didn't answer.

He bent down and kissed her and, going out the window, he let a spur drag across the ledge, scratching it. Then he dropped lightly to the ground. Hurrying into the trees where his horse was hidden, he swung up and rode out quietly. He was well away from the tavern when dawn broke over Red Cedar.

He was glad that Zack had got back from town so late. Always a sound sleeper, he was still in bed, lost to the world, when Ty got back to MQ, but Bernie was still up and curious. Ty met his questioning eyes with a blank stare. Bernie followed him to the corral.

There, where it was safe to speak, he said bluntly, "You'd better cough up. I'll have to tell whatever story you do."

"I'm telling no story."

"She wouldn't go for it?"

"I wouldn't ask her to."

96

Bernie swore bitterly. "The sheriff'll be here this morning. What are we going to say?"

"All he's interested in is the couple of hours before and after dark, last night. Up to eleven o'clock, the time it'd take me to get back here from Newkirk's if I'd been there. Well, we were here playing cards and wondering what was keeping Zack, and that's what we'll have to tell Sheriff Webster."

"He won't believe it this time."

"Then it's just my tough luck."

"What kept you so long at Evalyn's?" Bernie wondered, finally.

"We just talked. Maybe I'll have to leave here on the double, so we talked."

Bernie grinned but wiped the expression from his face when he saw Ty's eyes. "All right, and it's my bet you'll be taking it on the double. If you do, I'm going with you, and the hell with this dog's life."

Ty went to his own room in the old house, pulled off his boots and stretched out. Might just come off, he thought, depending on whether Webster made a public display of what Evalyn would tell him or chose to be discreet about it.

When he awakened, the room reeked with heat and its ancient odors. He distantly heard somebody talking and realized the sound had roused him from his nervous dozing. Again he was filled with apprehension, which he knew would come and go until he had been questioned by the sheriff. Maybe the man was here now.

When he walked down the creaking old stairs, he was not surprised to see Bernie standing in the yard in conversation with Webster. A momentary panic swept through Ty, then he steadied. Glancing through the window, he saw that the wagon was gone and knew that Zack had taken some of the salt out to distribute. He probably had not seen the sheriff. That looked like a good sign, it had to be one.

He was calm again when he stepped out into the yard. Webster saw him, said something to Bernie who moved off toward the barn. Then the sheriff, his face grave and impassive, came over to the porch.

"I wanted to see you alone, Maxon," Webster said quietly. "Bernie says you heard about Newkirk and what his woman claims. I stopped at Milliron's coming out, and they've cleared your brother. Bernie says you were here from supper time on, but I don't believe him."

Ty's heart began to race again. "Well, I was."

Webster cleared his throat and suddenly looked embarrassed. "This is a damned serious business, Maxon, so I've got to speak plain. You're covering up for somebody, and Bernie's covering up for you. Under the circumstances, I can see why you would."

"I don't know what you're driving at."

"I heard a different story a while ago. At Trahan's. She knew the sign pointed straight at you, so she told me."

Ty's mouth dropped open. "Who told you what?"

"Evalyn. That you spent the night there. With her."

"Then she's lying to help me. We're sort of engaged."

"I doubt she's lying," Webster said dryly. "Not only have I known her a long time, I trust her. And I looked around there a little to double check. There's a spur scratch on her window ledge. Fresh. There's plenty of horse sign in the woods closeby, fresh, too. Somebody was in her room by way of the window. Knowing Evalyn, I don't think it'd be anybody but the man she's in love with."

"I won't have a thing like that spread around!"

"It won't be spread," Webster answered quietly. "What time were you there?"

"All right," Ty said wearily. "About ten, I guess, till just before daylight. But, look! I'd rather take my chances than have that get out!"

"It won't go any farther. That's the time she said, so you couldn't have been at Ben Newkirk's."

"For God's sake, don't tell my brother," Ty said desperately. "He's in love with her, too."

"He's in the clear, so I won't have to see him at all."

There was a smile on Ty's mouth as he watched the sheriff ride out toward the Newkirk ranch. It had been a big gamble but he and Bernie had won.

Now he hoped the sheriff wouldn't work the truth out of Daycic or Jake. He wanted to take care of Jake Michaels, himself. Newkirk was small fry, as Lee had been, but Michaels had killed Kelsey. After him came Sam Milliron, who had done the shouting that night on Red Cedar Mountain.

13

Since his range joined the Newkirk spread on the east, making them neighbors, Ed Larkin rode over as soon as he heard what had happened to the old man. It was around ten in the morning when Ed topped the low, sage-studded rise and looked down on the shack where Ben and his wife had made their home for so many years; the drab, empty poverty it suggested depressed him.

He was tempted to turn back, because Daycie, with the way her eyes shifted over a man, always embarrassed him. But he saw at a glance that there were no extra horses about the place. Nobody had come to be with her, apparently not even Michaels, who had been more intimate with the Newkirks than anyone else. Ed felt sorry for the woman and rode on down the slope.

Daycie stood in the doorway when he came up, looking excited and yet disappointed by him. "I thought it was the sheriff," she complained. "Why don't he get here?"

"Takes a while," Ed said, touching his hat.

"Well, Ben ain't going to keep long, this weather."

Quickly, Ed said, "I wondered if there's something I could do for you. Any chores or anything?"

"I don't guess so," Daycie said. "Ben was over the range yesterday. Unless you want to dig a grave. I thought Jake would be over and he could do it, but he ain't showed up."

"Maybe he hasn't heard yet. I only did a while ago. I expect the sheriff'll claim the body, or I'd dig a grave. There'll have to be an inquest and all that. He might take Ben to town where he can form a jury."

"What on earth for?" Daycie said, her voice sharp. "All you got to do is look at Ben to know he's deader than hell."

"The law. They'll have to thresh it out."

"Nothing to thresh out," Daycie said, turning hostile.

99

"The Maxons come and killed him, that's all. I seen 'em."

"That's a serious thing to charge, Mrs. Newkirk. Are you sure it was them?"

"Who else could it be?" Daycie returned. "Ben was in the bunch that finished their father."

"That don't make them murderers," Ed said.

Suddenly Daycie stared off to the southeast, where the heat lay thick and dancing on the sage slope. "Maybe that's Webster," she said. "And it's about time."

Glancing in the same direction, Ed saw a rider top over the swell and come on. It did look like the sheriff, and though he wanted to leave Daycie, Ed knew he ought to wait to exchange greetings with Webster.

The sheriff wore a rock-hard face as he came up. He tipped a nod at Ed, saying, "Howdy, Larkin," then touched his hat to Daycie. "Bad news, Mrs. Newkirk, and I offer my sympathy. Now, now—" for Daycie began to cry. Ed wondered at that. She had been dry-eyed up to that moment, all the while she was talking about her dead husband. Webster swung out of the saddle.

Ed said, "I reckon I'd better go. If there's anything I can do—"

"Stick around," Webster said. "If she turns hysterical, I would as soon have help."

Ed stepped out of the saddle and trailed reins. The sheriff had moved onto the porch, was staring through the open door at the flood beyond. When he came up the steps, Ed saw the stain of pooled dry blood, thick with flies, and his throat worked. The sheriff didn't like to look at it, either.

"I heard what you told Peebles," Webster said. "Supposing you go over it again."

"Ain't much to go over," Daycie said, tossing her head and sniffing. "We'd just gone to bed, but I wasn't awake when they come. All I know is I woke up and somebody was shooting, out in the other room. When I got to the window, they were riding off, two of 'em. If it wasn't the Maxon boys, then I'm blind. When I went into the other room there was Ben down, dead already. I put him on the bed and went to Trahan's. They said they'd get you, so I come back."

"What made you feel it was the Maxons?"

"It looked like 'em."

"Well, it wasn't them. They've both got good alibis."

Daycie's face went slack. "They what?"

"They have proof they couldn't have been here when it happened."

"If it wasn't them," Daycie said weakly, "who was it?"

"I don't know, but your imagination played tricks on you because Ben was so afraid of the Maxon boys."

Ed was shocked at the look of fear that moved across Daycie's face although Webster, moving on into the house, didn't notice it. When the sheriff came back, he said grimly, "We've got to get him to the undertaker. You got a wagon or buckboard, Mrs. Newkirk?"

"Jake's got one. He'll do it."

"I'm going to see him next, so I'll arrange it. You come to town with him."

Walking down the steps, Webster looked around, trying to find fresh horse tracks, but in the tramped yard there was nothing apparent. Then he mounted and rode off, heading toward Michaels' place.

"If you're sure there's nothing I can do," Ed said, "I'll be going."

She looked at him with troubled eyes. "The Maxons had to kill him," she insisted. "They were the only ones who wanted to. Even Bernie thought they might."

"Bernie told you that?" Ed said sharply. "When?"

"Just yesterday, when he stopped by."

"The sheriff seems satisfied they had nothing to do with it. Goodbye, ma'am."

Ed had a deep uneasiness as he rode out, a feeling that something was very wrong. On the surface, even, it was a shocking, disturbing situation. It was easy to accept the theory that Lee had been shot for the money on him or the horses he had been driving, but there was nothing like that involved in the vicious attack on old Ben.

When he reached the rim of the little valley holding the Hawkeye headquarters, Ed couldn't help a feeling of pride at the contrast between his place and old Ben's hardscrabble layout. Hawkeye wasn't much larger; had been in the same class when Ed bought it. But repairs and additions had changed the whole atmosphere, and as he stopped his horse for a moment to look down upon his home he knew his hope of winning Evalyn had been the main reason for his self-denial and industry. That hope was gone now. He had known it ever since Ty Maxon returned.

Ed fixed his tardy noon meal and ate it, aware of a nagging restlessness brought back from Newkirk's. The sheriff had seemed satisfied that the Maxons were in the clear but, nonetheless, two mysterious killers were afoot in the Piute. The similarity between the Lee and Newkirk cases was too marked to be dismissed lightly. If somehow it had to do with the Maxon case, after all, Sam Milliron was also in line.

Suddenly Ed felt the urge to see Sam and talk it over with him, not to voice any suspicions, but to make sure that Sam was aware of the possible menace and guarded himself. He saddled a fresh horse and rode out.

Regardless of the change in his expectations, it was impossible for him to pass Trahan's without stopping. The noon stage had left, with the passengers who had eaten dinner there, when he rode up. There were no other vehicles or saddle horses in front. Angling in to the hitch-rack, he swung down and tied his horse. Evalyn was in the barroom when he entered, and Peebles was clearing the dining room table. He saw at a glance that Evalyn looked tired and tense.

Suddenly he was embarrassed without knowing why except that he had a feeling of intruding on her privacy. But he couldn't back out through the doorway, so he went on over to the bar.

In a quiet voice, she said, "Hello, Ed. Going somewhere?"

"Just down to Sam's. It's a hot day."

"They all are. Want a drink?"

"Too hot and too early." Then because he was sure she was worried about Ty he said, "I was at Newkirk's while the sheriff was there. He brushed Daycie's story aside. Said both the Maxons can prove they were somewhere else."

She glanced at him quickly. "Did he say how?"

"No. Just that Daycie let her imagination run away with her because she was afraid of them."

She looked relieved, and he was glad he had told her that. He still felt awkward and wanted to leave, but he asked, mainly because it was part of his routine, "How's Mamma?"

"You might go up and see her for a minute," Evalyn answered. "She's brooding over something today, and you can always cheer her up."

"Why, sure," Ed said and turned toward the stairs.

Mamma Trahan was in her sturdy rocker, but it was motionless. She sat apathetically, and her eyes were red. But they brightened when she answered his knock by calling out, and he stepped into the room. It was hot and stuffy, and he wondered how she could stand it up here day after day.

He closed the door, then went over to her, saying, "Why, what's the matter, Mamma? This heat got you frazzled?"

She shook her head on its thick, sweating neck. "It's everything, Ed. Just everything."

He knew that Mamma Trahan frequently needed a big dose of sympathy, but he could think of nothing to say to her.

Finally she said, "It's Evalyn. It ought to be you, Ed. I always wanted it to be you, and she's gone clean crazy."

"Now, now—!" Ed said hastily, aghast at the idea of her unloading something like that on him.

"I've got to talk, Ed," she insisted. "It's bad, and I've got to tell you, even if she is my own daughter. You can stop it, you've got to."

"Stop what?"

"I don't sleep, anymore, and last night—" Mamma took a handkerchief out of her apron pocket and wiped her eyes. "Last night I thought I heard a horse coming in. It wasn't in front, and when I looked out the side window I seen a man sneaking in from the woods. I thought it was a burglar, but it wasn't. The light was good enough that I know. It was Ty Maxon. Ed, he was in Evalyn's room from then till nearly daylight."

So that's his alibi, Ed thought. By God, I'll kill him. In a rough voice, he said, "What time was that?"

"Way late—two or three in the morning. But he was there a good two hours. Ain't that long enough? He's no good, Ed. He'll be the ruin of her. I'm telling you because you've got to stop it."

"If what I think is true," Ed said, "I'll stop it. Mamma, for God's sake don't let her know you told me, and don't you tell anybody else."

103

"I knew you'd do something. You won't want her now, but that's better than letting Ty Maxon ruin her completely."

"If Evalyn would have me right now I'd crawl to her on my hands and knees."

He was relieved to find, when he desecnded the stairs, that Peebles had taken over the bar, and Evalyn was not in sight.

He was filled with a sickness as he walked out to his horse, the facts Mamma told him making the murder even uglier than he had thought. Ty Maxon had no real alibi for last night. Daycie could have been right in her recognition in part, and the other man could have been Bernie. But Ed knew he could never tell anyone how he knew that, because Evalyn was more important to him than anything else.

He no longer wanted to go on to see Sam Milliron, yet it seemed all the more necessary now to warn him. There was a good chance that Ty Maxon was involved one way or another in both killings, that he had made ruthless use of Evalyn to protect himself when the second one endangered him too seriously. Ed wanted to kill him, and didn't see how he could live through another day without doing it.

He was hardly aware of the fact that he was on his horse, jogging south. Once he glanced over toward Red Cedar, the place where this had all started. Then he was lost again in his chill, sick thoughts until suddenly he realized that he had reached Sam's turn-off.

He found Sam home alone. Ed felt somewhat calmer, although he still did not know what he could do. He sat down across the table from Sam, who was finishing a cup of coffee.

He said, "Sam, you've got to face it. You're in danger till those killers are caught."

Sam shook his head. "It couldn't have been the Maxons, Ed. Nancy and Zack were together all day. And even if it was Ty and somebody else, Ty wouldn't be dumb enough to put his trademark on Ben's body. To my mind, somebody's using that old business to gain their own ends."

"But who? You've got to watch yourself till they're caught."

"Well," Sam said, "anybody's going to watch himself

104

with killers loose in the country. Don't you worry about me."

They sat quietly for a moment, and Sam continued, "Nancy's as scared for me as you are, Ed. She was in town only yesterday but rode back in today just to have something to do. This is hard country for a woman."

"I don't know anybody it's easy on."

"Or anything," Sam agreed. "But a woman suffers the worst. She's only half a person, and she's got to find the other half, and there's a mighty poor chance of that here. Say, you doing anything the rest of the day? I've got a ringy steer to dehorn, and he's too much for me. Seen him at the Pot Hole this morning. Aimed to have Nancy help, but she left before I got back this noon. And that fellow's going to be off somewhere by tomorrow."

"Glad to," Ed said and meant it, for he didn't like his own company just then.

The watering place called the Pot Hole lay east of the end of Red Cedar and not far from the north road where it came off the narrows. They found the steer Sam had in mind, roped it and relieved it of its mischievous horns. It was nearly dark when they got back to Sam's house, and Nancy met them as they came onto the porch.

She said, "Guess what. Daycie and Jake took Ben's body to town and went straight from the undertaker's to the parsonage and got married."

14

Jake Michaels had never been this afraid. He awakened with a splitting head, for he had been drinking since noon the day before, ever since he learned from the sheriff that the Maxon boys had cleared themselves of any connection with what had happened to old Ben. Jake planted his elbows on the hard tick of the bed, gave a shove and swung to a sit with his bare feet on the floor.

He could hear Daycie's heavy breathing behind him.

She had wanted to return to her own place for their wedding night, but he couldn't stand the thought of it, wished he had never come within a mile of there. So they had come to his place where, because of his chilling fear, he hadn't been able to give her what she expected.

He had felt the first acid bite of terror when, yesterday, he had looked up from his noon meal to see Sheriff Webster riding in. He had expected to be questioned, both because he was Ben's neighbor and had also been the one to send word to Webster when Loren Lee was shot. Even so, the sight of the officer and the star on his vest had completely unnerved him for a moment. All Webster wanted was for him to take Ben and Daycie to Piute, yet he had gone out of his way to say the Maxons had alibis for themselves, and Jake had seen serious trouble ahead. From the sheriff's chilly eyes he had gathered that he would have some difficult questions to answer when Webster was ready to ask them.

When he reached Newkirk's with his wagon, Daycie had been half crazy. He had told her the Maxon boys would catch the blame, and he was no smarter than she for he hadn't realized they might have perfect alibis. They had argued all the way to town about that, and about her insistence that he keep his promise to marry her immediately. When he tried to make her understand how queer that would look, she had threatened to accuse him of instigating the whole thing if the sheriff suspected her. So, even though he knew it was also risky, he had taken what seemed the less dangerous course.

This morning, with the Maxons removed as suspects, he knew he had not helped himself a bit. If suspicion settled on Daycie, she would break and spill the whole thing anyhow, and it would be worse for Jake because everyone knew she wasn't too accountable for her actions. They might put her in the asylum, but he'd hang because no jury would credit her with brains enough to try to frame the Maxons. Letting her scare him into marrying her had been the worst mistake of all; it would look like he engineered the whole thing to get hold of Ben's property as well as his wife.

While he got into his clothes, he looked down at her with distaste, remembering how she had pestered him the night long. He had never wanted to marry her, for the

106

other way he could have her when he wanted and not be bothered when he didn't. Yet she had him in her power now; he did not doubt that she would blat everything if he didn't handle her just right.

He didn't want to waken her and was very quiet when he moved out into the kitchen and went about getting himself some breakfast. He ate cold biscuits and meat, then drank a cup of lukewarm coffee. He could spend most of the day on the range, away from her, and he slipped out of the house. He was soon in the saddle.

He had not gone a hundred yards when he reined up, lifted himself on the stirrup leathers and threw a hard stare toward the brush running along the old dry wash to his right. He couldn't see anything unusual, but he felt tense. Was somebody over there; was he being watched by either the sheriff or one of the Maxon boys? His stare was so hard and fixed it seemed to penetrate the cover and actually discover someone hidden in the thicket.

He rode on, his thick legs still tense and trembling. Gradually he managed to persuade himself that he was just jittery. Lord knew he had been through enough since he found Daycie waiting for him in the cedars on Magnetic Hill. He cursed her silently, needing some outlet for his pent-up tensions. He reached his west springs and dismounted, not because there was anything wrong there but to work some of the tenseness out of him. He dropped flat to get a drink from the spring and when he raised up, his horse had its ears pricked and was looking toward something off in the east, the way they had come. Jake looked in the same direction, but a low butte cut off the view and he had no idea what had attracted the horse's attention.

Jake stood there with a foot resting on the spring fence, trying to face down his fear. Certain now that he was being stalked, the question was by whom. He got out his pipe, loaded and lighted it, but the smoke had a foul taste. He knocked it out, then put it back in his pocket. There was still a chance he was fooling himself. He swung to the saddle and rode on. The way forward began to lift into the Garnets. The natural craftiness of his mind came to grips with its problem. Farther up, where there were plenty of trees and rocks, he would have a chance to flush this thing into the open.

The sun, strengthening with the morning, began to heat

his back. He was used to the hot country, having been on the Piute most of his grown life after a boyhood spent with a jack-Mormon family south of the Escalante Desert. The deserts all bred tough creatures, and he was still alive with intentions of remaining so by whatever means.

He tried to think back and recapture some of the surging, confident excitement that had been in him when Daycie broached the matter of getting rid of Ben. His main desire had been to checkmate the Maxons, but he had also been excited about adding Ben's spread to his own. Even the thought of unimpeded access to Daycie had seemed attractive just then. But now he was conscious only of this uneasy feeling that he was being trailed.

He asked himself what it could be for, why the sheriff would think he might do something today to tie him in with what had happened yesterday. There wasn't anything left to do, as far as Jake was concerned. Ben was dead, the inquest had been yesterday with the murder charged to somebody unknown, and Ben had been buried in the town cemetary. If it was the sheriff following him, then it was that crazy trip to the parsonage had set the man's mind against him and Daycie, although there still was no reason to suppose that something might be gained by this stalking.

But suppose it wasn't Webster or one of his deputies. Jake faced it as he rode on stolidly. That left the Maxon brothers, and it seemed incredible that they would move so soon after getting off the hook about Ben. So probably it was nobody at all.

Jake had cattle all the way from the foothills to the summit of his part of the Garnets, and as he climbed higher on the gentle, broken plateau, he began to see them. It was always peaceful up here above the desert floor. Life seemed kinder although it was not. Jake nearly forgot his fear of being followed until he reached Roaring Spring, where mountain water boiled out of the base of a rock bluff. As he stopped he looked back and this time he saw a ridden horse, unmistakable although hardly more than a speck, back down the slope. His heart began to slam in his chest and his hand dropped to the grips of his gun. But for some reason the rider down there stopped the horse and sat still. Jake blinked his eyes, trying to clear his vision as if that was what was wrong, but there was no mistake. It was a horse and a man just waiting there, the way Jake had seen a wolf patiently wait for its prey.

Jake fought his nerves until they were a little quieter, then debated whether to ride back and demand an accounting. The fellow didn't mind being seen, apparently, so maybe he was just some drifter uncertain as to whether it was wise to come on. Then Jake made his decision and rode ahead. When he reached the end of the rim he again looked back, but the man was too far behind to be seen. Jake slanted to the right, got in under the formation where it broke down to a jagged boulder bed, and waited there, hidden among the rocks. He didn't draw his gun, but he was ready to do so.

He waited there half an hour, but nobody came along.

His nerves felt like hot wires again when he rode out cautiously. Either he was out of his mind or someone was playing cat and mouse with him. He could feel sweat run down his neck and ribs. This carried a sudden terrible significance. Somebody wanted him to sweat and he knew of only two men who would. Had they guessed he had tried to frame them through that half-witted woman? Did they have more in their craws now than the death of their father? Jake cursed himself for not forcing a showdown back there at Roaring Spring.

He began to backtrack himself. A little below the spring he found where the fellow had waited, beyond question, and afterward the man had ridden to his left up the slope. A bleak smile broke the stiffness of Jake's face. He had out-foxed the bugger who had swung on around, hoping to get ahead and cut him off. The horse was not hard to follow, and Jake set out in stubborn, hot-tempered pursuit, feeling he had every chance of turning the tables completely and putting a stop to this hunt. A Maxon up here, following him, could have but one intention, and he would be legally justified in killing that Maxon.

He rode warily, but the immediate country was such as to preclude a deadfall. Presently it grew thinly timbered again, then it topped out. The man had kept to the summit thereafter, going on, then a little later he had dropped back down. Jake smiled. Whoever it was, he had a fair knowledge of the route Jake usually followed on his daily riding, and he intended to reach the Duncan Creek watering before Jake did. Thus informed, Jake took a short cut, which would be safer for him.

Duncan Creek was a mountain brook that Jake had dammed long ago to build a pond. He approached it from upslope, keeping to the trees. There were a few steers in the open meadow below him, and they looked undisturbed. He jumped the horse across the brook above the pond and went on a distance. There was nobody at the pond or in the trees on this side, and he grew puzzled again. Finally he steeled himself and rode into the open, going down to the pond. There were fresh tracks in the mud where a horse had just drunk. Then Jake saw something in the trees on the other side of the meadow, jerked out his gun and shot at it. A steer cut out of the cover, kicking up its heels.

Cursing, Jake holstered the weapon, completely unnerved again, suddenly feeling very alone and helpless. But he could no longer write it off to nerves and imagination. Something was up, an extremely deadly business, and he had to meet it to stay alive. He was tempted to ride for home, but he knew that would be useless. If he had to have a fight, it had better be now while he was warned, expecting it. Loren Lee hadn't been given any such chance. He set out doggedly on the course he usually followed to Magnetic Hill, the last watering on his range.

He rode to the base of Magnetic Hill without incident. There was no one in sight as he came in to the waterhole. But someone had been there. It wasn't horse tracks he discovered this time. Someone had used a stick or his finger to draw a crude symbol in the smooth mud by the water. Jake recognized it at once—a hangnoose. He walked back to his horse and sagged against it, sick.

He looked up the slope of the hill and saw Ty Maxon up there against the cedars.

Jake jerked up his pistol and shot, throwing himself into the protection of the horse as it wheeled, then the horse broke away and went thundering off. Jake fired again at the hill before he realized Maxon was no longer in sight. He threw himself flat, watching with straining eyes, expecting a return fire that did not come. Had it been an illusion? Of course not. He pressed himself flat, his lungs pulling in great gulps of air. When he looked the other way, his horse had vanished into a draw, panicked by his shooting and the way he had lunged against it to conceal himself. He was afoot, and Ty Maxon was on top of the

110

hill. This was the final moment of the decade since he had sent a bullet singing into Kelsey. It seemed now that he had always known it would come.

Jake lay flattened there a long while, staring at the empty hillside until his eyes stung and tears scalded them. Why didn't the man make his fight; it was too intensely cruel to drag it out this way. They hadn't done that with Lee; with him it had been quick and final. Had they learned somehow he was the one who shot Kelsey down? Lee, Newkirk or Milliron could have told them. Jake lay sweating in his resentment of that. Somebody had to drop Kelsey. They thought he was a horse thief who needed hanging, and he was getting away from them, not surrendering. Anyhow, Ben Newkirk had pointed the finger at Kelsey, not him—Jake Michaels. Actually, Jake was the only one justified in being up there on the mountain since it was his horses that had been stolen.

Jake found himself wanting to vomit. The area about him was completely exposed, and the only way he could protect himself at all was to lie flat like this. The sun was already hot sheet iron pressed to his back, and sweat boiled out of him. He would have a heat stroke if it went on long enough. Maybe that was the play. A heat stroke could kill a man if he didn't get prompt attention.

Despair seemed to drain some of the fear from him, some of the caring what happened to him. Finally he raised himself up slightly, hoping that if Maxon was hidden up there he would be tempted to shoot, disclosing his position. But nothing happened through long, hot moments. Jake weighed the situation again and again. At last, moved by desperation, he shoved to a rocking stand. He stared at the empty hill side with eyes that barely saw it. He invited attack but no attack came. He had a sudden feeling of dignity and contempt. He turned his back on the hill and started walking toward home.

The horse, because of the dragging reins, had gone into the draw a ways, then stopped. But when Jake tried to approach it, it wheeled away. He cursed it, half crying. Everything all at once was too difficult to bear. The horse stopped again, and this time, because he coaxed it gently, he came up to it without trouble. He felt better when he had leather between his legs again.

He came out of the draw onto the desert, and it was

completely empty except that far forward in the haze he could faintly discern the trees that marked his place, his home which he had never expected to see again. He knew with dead certainty what he would do when he got there.

Daycie was up, frowsy and fretful. She looked at him accusingly when he came in, as if she knew he had left so early just to get away before she woke up. But when she saw the look on his face and the heavy dust on his clothes, she let out a cry.

"Jake, what's the matter? Something happen to you?"

"Everything's fine," he said with a vicious savagery. He lunged on into the bedroom. When she followed him in, he had pulled a cowhide trunk from under the bed and dug into it. He had a roll of bills in his hand, which he stuffed into his pocked as he rose.

"What you going to do with that money, Jake?" she asked.

"None of your damned business."

She watched him with dull eyes that slowly brightened with understanding. "You still scared?" she asked tonelessly. "You pulling out, Jake?" When he didn't answer, she screamed, "Not without me you ain't, Jake!"

He shoved her with the flat of his hand as he went past to the other room.

She was on him like a wildcat. He cuffed her again, knocking her off her feet. She lay blubbering on the floor as he stared down at her, seeing nothing but hot, female flesh that now was repulsive to him. Why had he ever desired her, even those nights back there in old Ben's barn? He didn't blame the old man. Maybe Ben just got so he wilted every time he looked at her.

"Since you want to know," he said heavily, "I'm going, Daycie. I'll put this place up for sale when I hit Piute, and the agent can send me the money if anybody buys it."

"Jake, they'll catch and hang you sure, because I'll tell 'em."

"Not if you don't get there first," Jake said. "Because I'm telling Webster it was you, that I just found out, and he won't have anything but an idiot's word to tie me into it. After what happened today, I'll take my chances on that."

"Jake, don't you run out on me! Everything I done was for you as much as me!"

112

He laughed and walked out. He was at the corral gate, unfastening it to enter and rope a fresh horse, when something drilled into the back of his head. He never knew what it was.

15

The southbound stage was on time. As it unloaded out front, Evalyn made a quick count of the six passengers from the dining room window and signaled to Minnie, who stood in the kitchen doorway, by holding up five fingers then a single one. Minnie faded back into the kitchen. Peebles was unhitching the stage horses. Evalyn crutched back into the bar.

This was a routine that went on every day, the only thing that changed was the weather as the seasons passed, and right now was the end of the hottest day of that summer. The trip down from Alta had been long and dusty, the passengers were glum and thirsty, and until Peebles put supper on the table trade at the bar was brisk. Finally they were going again, on toward Piute, and suddenly Evalyn had an overpowering desire never to see their like again.

Maybe it was the day's wearing heat, but she was not happy that Ty and she had consummated their love. That in itself had been precious, but she wished she had not had to tell Webster of that most intimate experience, particularly that it had to be distorted into a substantial lie. But it was worth the price, and the truth had come out yesterday when the man-crazy woman at the foot of the Garnets had killed Jake Michaels and given herself up. If she hadn't protected Ty the way she did the truth might never have emerged, and he'd be the one in jail in Piute right now. She didn't know the whole story yet, having heard only a few details from Rex Thornton when he stopped in for a meal at noon.

Peebles closed the dining room, but she told him she was

feeling all right and would tend the bar that evening. He disappeared, and she swung herself onto her stool and spread before her on the bar the Territorial Enterprise that had come in with the northbound stage. But she had barely started reading it when somebody stopped in front, a rider, and Sam Milliron came in. She wondered at once if something new had developed, but he didn't seem excited.

She said, "Evening, Sam. Going up to see Ed?"

"I've got to go up to the Roaring Horse," Sam answered, as she set up the bar bottle and a shot glass. "I owe Bot Hames some work, and he's gelding colts tomorrow."

"Why don't you take Nancy?"

"She didn't want to go, but she'll be all right. It's sure a relief to know who killed Ben. That's a funny thing, how anyone'd admit to that yet claim it was somebody else who shot Jake. Proves she's clean crazy."

Evalyn gave him a baffled glance. "I thought she gave herself up for killing Jake."

Sam shook his head. "I went over there with the sheriff. She says Jake was running out on her, aiming to turn her in for shooting Ben, which she admits she did. But she insists it was somebody hid in the barn that shot Jake in the back of the head at the corral. This time she ain't trying to say who. They'll send her to the insane asylum, and I'm glad that's all. This world ain't been very good to Daycie. Ben or Jake either one thought more of a horse."

"My Lord," Evalyn said, shaking her head. "Do you suppose she killed Lee, too?"

"That was a pretty plain case of robbery. She killed Ben to get Jake, and when he learned what she'd done he tried to duck out of it. So she killed him, no matter what she claims. He was leaving her. There was a big roll of money in his pocket."

Sam dropped a coin on the bar to pay for his drink and went out. Looking through the window, she saw Ty and Bernie ride up just as Sam reached his horse. It was the first time, she supposed, that Ty and Sam had encountered each other since Ty's return, and she saw Sam stiffen, his features turning impassive. Bernie walked over and talked with Sam a moment, but Ty stayed by his

114

horse, seeming to pay no attention to them. Then Sam mounted and rode on. Ty and Bernie came in.

She waited for Ty's eyes to find her and convey his reassurance, his love, but he only gave her a smile and a nod. Bernie's sun-brown face wore an expansive grin as they tramped to the bar. Reaching into his pocket, he withdrew and dropped several coins on the bar top, his smile centering on them fondly.

"We're buying the joint, Evalyn!" he announced. "Lock the doors!"

Evalyn's eyes widened when she saw the five gold eagles he had dropped there so carelessly. "What on earth?" she gasped. "Did you stick up a bank?"

"Won a bet," Bernie told her proudly. "One hundred pesos." He had been drinking already, she realized, which was why his eyes stayed so bright. "Ty bet it couldn't be done, and I done it. One shake of the goddam tree."

"That's enough," Ty said sharply. "He's lit, and I tried to leave him home, Evalyn. But he had to come."

"You're damned right," Bernie agreed. "You can spark her later, but right now we're gonna celebrate. Evalyn, set up the best you've got and plenty of it."

"This place is not a joint," Evalyn returned, "and you're not buying it, Bernie. How about some supper? I think there's enough left."

"A good idea," Ty agreed.

Bernie laughed. "Come on! Let's have a drink to MQ."

"It's got cause to celebrate?" Evalyn asked, suddenly very curious as to what he was so elated about.

"It sure has. Maxon and Quick! When it decides to go to town, it gets there."

"Then by all means let's have the drink," Evalyn said. "But only one, Bernie."

Puzzled and growing concerned, Evalyn joined them at the back corner table. Although he again gave her his quick, intimate smile, Ty remained quiet until he and Bernie had each had a drink from the bottle Bernie had brought from the bar. Then he began to relax from the tension she sensed in him. Whatever had worried him, the drink had made it look less bad. She didn't protest when Bernie filled the glasses again, leaving that up to Ty, who made no objection.

115

"Is that hundred dollar bet any of my business?" she asked.

"Why not?" Bernie said, and she wondered at the quick warning on Ty's features. "I bet that if Jake married Daycie she'd kill him—though not the way she did."

That was coarse and cheap, and she knew Bernie had not meant to tell her the truth. But Ty realized she was puzzled and offended. Tartly, he said, "Old big mouth, there. The bet was on a poker hand, Evalyn. We were both bluffing, and he beat me with a pair of sevens. He's been crowing about it ever since."

"Shucks," Bernie said. "The one I told was funnier. Say, Sam said he was going up to the Roaring Horse, and poor Nancy must be home all alone. Why don't we go get her and have a party?"

Knowing how Nancy felt about Bernie Quick, Evalyn said quickly, "How about Zack? Why didn't he come along?"

"He's been over on the east vegas the last two-three days," Bernie answered. "We thought he'd be home today, but he never showed up. That boy's all work and no play. Don't you have anything to do with him, Evalyn. Stick to old Ty. He's fun."

It bothered her that he assumed she was only a play-mate of Ty's. Yet how did she know she was anything more? They kept drinking, and she realized that Bernie was still bent on making a night of it here, Ty now offering no objection. They knew she never permitted drunkenness here, and all at once she wondered if Ty's respect for her had been lowered, since that night.

If only he knew how much it had cost her, what her mother had said to her the night before. She had a sudden, crushing realization that she didn't know this man she loved at all, that the love was for a boy out of her past. She had to know more, particularly what Bernie was gloating over that Ty wanted to keep hidden. They had toasted MQ, which was growing rapidly, and all at once suspicion wormed into her mind.

"I wonder what will happen to those two ranches," she said, "with the men gone and Daycie locked up."

The look in Ty's eyes told her she had hit the mark.

Bernie was too drunk to notice the pointedness of her question. He said, "They're hers, even if she did murder

116

to get 'em. The law goes that way unless some other heir can upset it, and as far anybody knows Ben and Jake had no kin. But with her mind addled and her going to the asylum, the court'll likely put her property in the hands of a custodian."

"You're quite a lawyer."

Bernie missed the tartness of that, too. "We seen the Piute lawyer today because we want that range so we can keep the Belkirk herd. Somebody's got to take care of the stock already on it, and the lawyer's going to try for a deal so we can, in return for running some of our own stuff on it. Later, when things are settled, we can either buy or lease."

"So that's the reason for the celebrating." Evalyn felt a small shudder between her shoulders. She lifted the whisky Bernie had poured for her at the start but which she had barely tasted. "Another toast to MQ! It's growing by leaps and bounds. And, boys, what next?"

Ty's eyes snapped a glance at her. "You sure like to run off at the mouth, Bernie," he snapped.

"Why not? I feel good."

In a mollifying way, Ty said, "Somebody's got to take over the Michaels and Newkirk ranches, Evalyn. We got to talking about it and figured it would be a good deal all around if we did. Since Daycie's a mental case, we wondered what the legal angles would be and found out. That's all there was to it except old Charlie Goodnight, there, had some drinks and started feeling like a cattle king."

"I want to be a cattle king," Bernie said goodhumoredly. "And you do, too. What's the matter, Evalyn? Don't you want to be a cattle queen?"

"I've got my hands full with this place," Evalyn said.

After a few more drinks, the irritation between Ty and Bernie was gone, but Evalyn was miserable and depressed. She wanted Ty to ask her to marry him, although she had supposed he was taking that for granted the way some men did, not realizing how important it was to a woman to have it spoken and definite. Why did he make no effort to help her feel better about it?

The night had come but fortunately, since they were here and bent on drinking, nobody had stopped from the road to be put up. The back of the building grew quiet, and she knew Peebles and his wife had gone to bed.

117

There was no rocking chair sound from her mother's room upstairs. She wanted Ty and Bernie to leave so she could be by herself.

It seemed forever before Ty said, "Let's hit the trail, Bernie."

"We ain't come near spending the hundred bucks."

"The devil with that. Evalyn looks like she's ready to fall out of her chair."

So he had noticed, after all.

Bernie glanced at the wall clock, instantly contrite. "Lordy, nearly ten o'clock, when all good girls are in bed."

"Go on," Ty said impatiently. "I'll be out in a minute."

Bernie looked knowing and came to his feet. He reeled as he walked toward the door and went out. Looking after him, Evalyn knew that brash impulses still drove him, and she wondered in continuing dejection where he and Ty would go from here.

Lowering his voice, Ty said, "I couldn't shake him, but I'd like to come back. May I?"

"But it's late."

He smiled. "For us?"

It would have been kinder had he struck her, for his eyes more than his words told her clearly that he expected to come again to her bedroom, that to him that had become a regular privilege, a thing he would expect to keep happening whenever he felt the need. Had he taken her in his arms first or simply told her he loved her it might have made a difference. At is was the words hit her cold, destroying her last illusion about him and the depth of his feeling for her and leaving her with an awful knowledge that this was not the boy she had known so long ago or the man that boy should have become.

"So you think you've got it all staked out," she said bitterly. "A big, growing ranch and an easy woman. There's something I'd better tell you, Ty Maxon. My mother saw you come and leave the other night. Moreover, she told Ed Larkin, hoping he'd put a stop to it. Apparently she has the same opinion of me you do. She warned me last night, afraid I'd let you come back. I didn't want to tell you, but now I see I should."

She had not expected it to drive so deeply into him. His weight sank back in the chair, he went limp all over. "My God," he breathed.

118

"It frightens you? Why? Men are supposed to do things like that if they can get away with it. You did. You ought to be proud of yourself."

"It's you I'm thinking of!" he said angrily. "How could she do that to you? And how did she know it was me?"

"She gave the exact time you came and left."

"Jesus," he whispered.

"She doesn't know I lied to Webster," Evalyn said harshly. "But I want the truth about something, now. MQ's made out awfully well from these killings. It buys Lee out and he is murdered. Michaels and Newkirk are killed, and MQ promptly arranges to acquire their range. I saw the way you looked at Sam Milliron outside, tonight. Ty, I want an honest answer. You had something to hide when you came to me the other night, didn't you? And I did just what you hoped I'd do!"

A bitter, driving anger was coming up in him. "I gave you the truth then. Daycie Newkirk's confessed she killed Ben. A crazy woman's attempt to get the man she wanted."

"But how crazy is she in her claim that somebody else shot Jake Michaels from inside the barn?"

She had never before seen animal eyes in a human being, and after that she knew for sure. The horror of it stopped the flow of words she had been hurling at him, it held her fixed where she sat.

After a long moment in which those eyes burned into hers, Ty rose from the table. His voice wasn't the one she knew when he said, "Don't say things like that to any-body else. Don't let your mother make me trouble, either. I mean it." Then he went out.

She knew her thoughts and emotions had been arrested by the same bullet that crippled her body, fixing them as of that long ago moment, stopping her growth and con-fining her to a set and narrow course. A decade had passed, and none of it had been real. If only she had opened her eyes to Ed.

She felt a jab of fear as she thought of Ed. In her de-spair she had not realized that, in telling Ty that Ed knew his alibi was false, she might have endangered Ed's life. For she was sure from what she had seen in Ty's eyes that he was a killer. She reached for her crutches and got onto them. She thumped her way down the back hall to the Peebles' door. She rapped urgently.

Peebles called drowsily, "What is it?"

"I want my buggy! Quickly!"

"This time of night? Something wrong?"

"Hurry, I tell you!"

Peebles appeared in a moment, half-dressed, bewildered but no longer questioning. By the time he had brought the buggy up front, Evalyn was waiting there. He helped her in. Aware of his mounting alarm, she said more moderately, "I've got to see Ed Larkin, that's all. You go back to bed."

"Can't I go——?"

"No."

She drove like the wind, taking the old north road toward the lake. It seemed hours before, far forward, she saw the benighted huddle of Hawkeye headquarters, serene in the starlight. In her turmoil she had imagined that Ty might come here at once to silence Ed and protect himself. She called out as she drove into the yard at a clatter.

Ed was a few moments in appearing in the doorway. She saw that he had pulled on his pants but nothing else. Regardless, when he recognized her he came off the porch in a bound and rushed to the side of the buggy.

"What is it, Evalyn?" he asked.

She told him every bit of it, confirming what her mother had said, not sparing herself for her folly.

"You're released from your manacles, Ed," she concluded. "You don't have to protect me, now. He'll kill you if he can and it'll be my fault. I know he means to kill Sam Milliron. Webster's probably still in Piute. I'd go but you can get there faster. Tell him I lied to him."

"But, Evalyn——!"

"He already knows Ty was in my room. He just doesn't know that I lied about the time. That's all you've got to tell him. Even if you're willing to take your chances, Ed, there's Sam. Webster's got to be told. I helped protect a criminal, and I'm guilty, too."

Desperately, he said, "You didn't know."

"I knew I was lying to the law, Ed."

After a long thought, he said, "All right, I'll go. If Webster kept the other under his hat, I don't reckon he'd drag it out just to punish you for lying to him."

"Just hurry, Ed," she pleaded. "I don't care what happens to me."

120

"But I do. I always will."

Her eyes brimmed with tears. "Thank you, Ed."

He kept his horse beside the speeding buggy while she returned home, then went on, fading finally in the far starshine. Before she called out for Peebles to help her alight, Evalyn sat for a moment staring after Ed, her heart warming with something she had never before felt for him. Then she swung her gaze very slowly toward the distant bulk of Red Cedar Mountain. In her heart was a prayer for the boy who had been killed up there, that night, with Kelsey Maxon.

16

Bernie knew from the glowering way Ty came out the door and down the steps that something was very wrong. He had untied his horse and mounted while he waited, swaying a little because of the whisky he had consumed that afternoon and evening. He supposed that Evalyn had spoken her mind to Ty about this little celebration and that Ty resented it, as any man would resent that kind of lecturing from a woman.

When he was lit, the world took on a new color for Bernie. Dangers seemed trivial, difficulties easy to overcome, his every desire not only possible but probable of fulfillment. He achieved in those intervals a warm, demonstrative love for his fellow men, a tolerance he assumed to be returned, feelings of which he was not sincerely capable when sober. He had no idea that his own broad talk through the evening had anything to do with Ty's temper.

Without a word Ty swung onto his horse, and they headed south along the stage road. By degrees Bernie grew aware that he was included in Ty's wrath. At first he disdained it, then because Ty was the closest he had ever had to a friend he became uneasy.

"I reckon I let my tongue come loose at both ends,"

he said finally. "But hell, Evalyn's a good sport and your woman, and I figured she was one of us."

"No more," Ty said. "She just made that plain."

"How do you mean?"

"I mean," Ty said savagely, "that you had no cause for feeling so damned good tonight. I took too much for granted with her, and she just told me two people know I don't have a real alibi for the night Ben Newkirk was killed." He swore. "The one thing I had nothing to do with at all."

"My God," Bernie said. "Who knows?"

"Her mother saw me coming and going, that night, and knows what time it was. The old tallow-head told Ed Larkin."

"Criminy. But Daycie's confessed to killing Ben."

"While claiming somebody else killed Jake. If Webster finds out what Larkin knows, he's apt to pin both jobs on me. Because of Lee. Damn it, I wish you'd never set out to use that half-wit."

"Sure, blame me," Bernie hooted. "You were sure hot to get on Jake's tail the minute you thought you could get away with it."

"The question's what to do about it," Ty said, sounding suddenly tired. "If that alibi is proved false, it'll set up a powerful case of circumstantial evidence against me. I'll look more guilty than if I'd actually killed old Ben."

"Too?" Bernie said very softly, reminding him. When Ty said nothing, he went on musingly, "Well, if Evalyn's turned on you, it wouldn't do any good to fix Larkin, for she'd still talk. What the hell? If things get too hot, we can wind up our business in these parts fast. There's a get-away stake buried up there under that old chimney on Red Cedar. We could sure have us a time spending that."

"I'm not leaving while Sam Milliron's still alive."

"I said we'd wind up our affairs," Bernie answered cheerfully. "I've got a little thing on my mind to take care of, too."

He refused to worry, although the night air and the jolting talk had partly sobered him. The idea of leaving with Ty, well-heeled as they could be, began to take root. For days, recently, the old deadness had been on him,

122

the craving for strong excitement like a thirst that nothing could cut. He had thought up the deal whereby they cleared the way to more range, but the physical steps had been taken by others so that he was still unsatisfied.

When they reached the place where they usually turned off across the range to MQ, Bernie said, "Look, you go on. I'll be along pretty soon."

"Now what?"

Bernie laughed. "Do I poke my nose into your love affairs?"

Ty looked puzzled, dubious, then shrugged. "Damn you, don't you make matters worse."

"What I've got in mind don't have a thing to do with our troubles. Don't worry about that."

Ty turned off, and Bernie rode straight on. He thought he was completely sober now, filled with something more pleasant than mere booze. What difference did it make how a man got his satisfaction as long as he got it? If the deal, the way they had planned it, was going to backfire again, the thing to do was make new plans. That old haul Kelsey had cached on Red Cedar had never left his mind, and he had chafed at Zack's righteous attitude about it. It alone was worth as much as the ranch they were trying to put together and a lot easier to shove across a bar, gaming table or into the palm of a woman.

What a blessing it would have been if he had known of that money's existence a long time ago. His life had been hardly bearable when Ty and Zack were here as boys; after they left it had become unendurable. But he'd had to stand it because he had no way of getting away. His father never gave him a dime, nothing but the back of his hand and the sharp end of his tongue. If he had known about that treasure, he would have killed Thurm Quick and taken off for the far side of way yonder.

As he drew closer to her place, his thoughts began to center on Nancy Milliron. He remembered once when she was no more than twelve or thirteen, but with woman signs beginning to show through her clothes, when he had come upon her on Red Cedar, catching her dismounted so she couldn't run off from him. He'd been around eighteen and had never had a woman, not even a squaw, and something had exploded in him. She fought him like a wildcat and finally laid him cold with a rock.

123

He had never forgotten or forgiven her, for he had seen himself as a suffering boy she could have relieved handily instead of turning high and mighty.

When he reached the Milliron turn-off, he was surprised to see lamplight in the front window. For a moment he was afraid Sam had changed his mind and come home. But probably not. Women alone in a ranchhouse at night sometimes left a light burning because they were nervous. He remembered also that Nancy liked books, read a lot of them. He made no effort to be quiet as he rode in, and as he neared the house he called a disarming hallo he hoped she would mistake for her father's announcement of his return.

It worked. As he rode into the yard he saw her figure, still clad in day dress, framed in the lamplight of the doorway. But she had seen it was not her father and stood ready to step back and close the door hastily. Bernie smiled to himself, for he thought he knew how to take some of the ginger out of her.

She wasn't sure who he was until he rode up to the edge of the porch. He saw her stiffen, but she was too proud to show him any fear.

"What are you doing here, Bernie Quick?" she called across the porch. He knew she was going to move back inside in a minute.

"Don't look so much like a scared cat, Nancy," he returned. "I just want to see Sam."

His vigor coursed in him as he watched her hesitate, and he knew that he didn't want to stay on the Piute any longer. It wouldn't take much more to put Ty in the same frame of mind, and all he had to do was supply the extra impetus. He would finish this little visit, then go home and tell Ty what he had done, and Ty would be more than willing to ride. They would go up to the old Maxon cabin and get the money. Sam Milliron was at the Roaring Horse ranch. They could stop there and take care of that and still be right on their way to far parts. Bernie wanted to do that almost as much as he wanted to humble this snippety girl.

"He's asleep," Nancy said finally.

"You better call him, then. It's important."

"Tell me and I'll tell him."

124

"If I have to roll him out myself, I will." Bernie swung down from the saddle.

She had taken a step backward but still had not closed the door when he looked at her again. But she was openly frightened now, wanting to slam the door on him but kept from it by her wonder as to what had really brought him.

"He's not here," she admitted finally. "He's up at the Roaring Horse, and you can find him there if it's that important."

He got his foot in the door before she could close it. Although she pushed with all her might, he shoved her back and stepped in. Then he closed the door, keeping his eyes on her, seeing there was no gun close that she could sweep up. He moved forward so that he hemmed her in the deep end of the room, away from the inner doorway. She stood staring at him, terrified, yet contemptuous and lovely.

"You knew that all the time," she said bitterly.

He laughed.

"You're drunk, Bernie. You'd better go before you do something you'll be sorry for tomorrow."

He smiled at her. Of all the excitements leaping through him, her fear aroused the most pleasant. "Tomorrow," he announced, "I won't give a damn what anybody in this country thinks. I never did much, anyhow. Nancy, I come over to say goodbye, that's all."

She was surprised. "You mean you're leaving?"

"Sorry to hear it, honey?"

"Don't call me that, Bernie Quick. And you know I'm not sorry. You've said goodbye, now go. Please."

"What's the rush? If Sam ain't here to object, there's no reason why you and me can't have a little farewell party, Nancy."

She said nothing.

He had lots of time. She knew what was going to happen, which was almost as good as the happening would be. But he would have to watch her. The first time he had ever been alone with her, she had shown some remarkable capabilities.

He said, "Set down, Nancy. It won't hurt you to talk a while."

With some uncertainty she sank down on the edge of

a chair, the cornered look never leaving her pretty eyes. He took off his hat and put it on the table, then used his foot to hook another chair around. When he sat down he was arranged so he could keep her penned in. She saw that, her eyes appraised every little move he made.

He said, "I always was sorry you wouldn't let me be friends."

"I was never the kind of girl you wanted for a friend, and you know it."

He chuckled. "Which kept you kind of lonesome too, didn't it?"

"I preferred that, believe me. Bernie, you can find your kind everywhere. Why have you always pestered me?"

"Not your kind, Nancy. The woman makes a difference, who she is, what she is. You're rare."

"I suppose I should thank you, but I'm not flattered."

"You're pure. I ain't ever had a pure woman, Nancy, not one."

Her head came up. "I don't know what kind of base pleasure you're getting from this, but I'm asking you to leave."

Bernie stared at her, his eyes burning, thinking about what he had just said. He had never expressed it before, not even to himself, but that was it. It wasn't only that she was pretty, for he had had pretty women, plenty of them. It wasn't her unwillingness because he had coaxed a few into it, too. It was her untouchedness and the fact that he had never possessed a woman no other man had had before him. She had this qualification, he wanted it, he meant to have it.

When she saw that he wouldn't go, she seemed resigned, hoping that possibly, without drinking to keep the edge on him, his mood would change. She sat quietly, her eyes never leaving him, ready to move fast if she had to do it. Every little tension she betrayed delighted him.

"Is Ty Maxon going with you?" she asked presently.

"It's likely, and I hope so. He's the only friend I ever had."

"That was your own fault. You've always been a bad egg, which was also your choice, entirely."

"You didn't grow up with my old man."

"That's only your excuse, not your reason. What hap-

126

pened to Ty is only his excuse, because Zack went through the same experience and came out entirely different."

He gave her a brittle stare. "What's the meaning behind that?"

Coolly, Nancy said, "I think Ty killed Loren Lee, Jake Michaels and Ben Newkirk. It's probable that you helped him."

A bright anger leaped into his eyes. "That's dangerous talk, Nancy."

She shrugged. "If you get away with what you came here for, I want you to kill me."

It was a moment before he got hold of his surging emotions. Bitterly, he said, "It don't matter what you think, and I won't kill you. I want you to have to live with it."

"Why do you hate me so, Bernie—and everybody else?"

"I've never seen cause to do otherwise."

"Apparently not."

He wished she hadn't started him thinking along lines like that; his head began to ache. She had been too smart for him, the edge was going and he was beginning to let down.

Savagely, he said, "The hell with your why, why, why. What difference does it make? A man's what he is, and that's all there is to it. A woman's what she is. You're pure, I'm dirty."

"And you want to make me dirty."

"I'm going to."

He rose and moved toward her. To his surprise, she didn't move, simply watched him with unchanging eyes. For some reason he stopped halfway to her, staring down. If she would try to run or fight him the way she had up on the mountain, the excitement would boil through him again. Now, especially after the whisky, the deadness was seeping through him. As always, that feeling frightened him. Then an idea, bright and thrilling, burst in his mind.

He said, "Maybe you're right about Lee and the others. You know who that makes next, don't you?"

"Of course I know. My father."

"Nancy, it happens I seen Sam at Trahan's and know where he is, tonight. I got to wondering just how much

127

you care for your old man, since you think it was wrong for me to hate mine. Ty and me are leaving tonight. What we do between now and then won't make matters a bit worse for us. I could get Sam off."

"I see. Now you want me to offer myself to you."

"You bear that kind of love for Sam Milliron?"

"I love him."

"Then how about it?"

She shook her head, less in negation than in wonder. "Bernie, you almost make me sorry for you. You want the whole world to be as rotten as you are so you won't have to be reminded of what you are. As to my buying my father's life, he doesn't want to live that bad, and I wouldn't want him to."

Baffled, he was tempted to move upon her physically again, but all at once a sound came through the night. He stared at Nancy, saw her intent listening, convincing him that he had not imagined that call of approach all rangemen used. Somebody was coming here, maybe Sam was coming home after all, and frustration rolled through Bernie.

"If that's your father—!" he said hoarsely.

"You'll kill him?"

"You're damned right I will. That day you used a rock on me on Red Cedar Mountain, I swore I'd take it away from you. I'm still going to."

A horse came up in front. A voice rang out. "You still up, Sam?" Bernie's knees went limp.

"You going to kill *him?*" Nancy said and smiled.

"Keep quiet about what I said to you or, by God, I will."

She walked contemptuously to the door and threw it open. "Come in, Zack," she called out.

She didn't need to say a thing. The look on her face, as Zack walked in and saw Bernie, did it all. Bernie stood dazed by the unexpectedness of it, watching the fury that broke the surprise of Zack's face.

"What are you doing here, Bernie?" he rapped out.

"I come to see Sam. How did I know he wasn't home?"

Zack didn't believe him. He looked back at Nancy and had his suspicions confirmed. To Nancy, he said, "Sam isn't here?" When she shook her head, he added, "Get

128

out of here, Bernie. Right now. We'll have a talk about this and some other things when I get home."

"Don't you get high handed with me, Zack," Bernie warned.

He struck out as Zack came toward him, but the blow didn't land. Something smashed into his face and he went down. He didn't even know it when he hit the floor.

17

It was unbelievable that he should be standing with Nancy in his arms and her silently crying against his chest. Wrenching emotions filled both of them. He had stepped into the room to see Bernie as a total stranger, a vicious creature of the desert, and Nancy's eyes told him plainly what she had been through. He had a hand on the soft hair at the back of her head, so fine and fragrant, and he wanted to touch his lips to the top of her head, which barely reached his chin.

"I brought you here," she whispered, "with the picture of you I held in my mind while he was threatening me. It drew you to me."

"Maybe," he said, "but I wanted to see your father. I didn't hear about Jake Michaels till this evening at Ashton's. Something's wrong, Nancy, mighty wrong. I wanted to talk to Sam about it."

She stepped back and looked up, her eyes glinting with tears. She made an embarrassed smile. "I'm sorry I let go, but he made it so terrifying."

"You're all right?"

"Yes. He wanted it to be slow and painful. I hate to tell you this, but something's happened that's made him completely reckless. He said he and Ty are leaving the country tonight. He admitted they're involved in the killings. I don't know what's frightened them. But he wanted to get even with me for never having anything to do with him. And—apparently Ty intends to kill my father. They

129

know he's up at the Roaring Horse ranch. They saw him at Trahan's."

"Dear God," Zack said, after a moment.

She went on to tell him all that Bernie had divulged, although he had known much of it in an intuitive way already. The east vegas, where he had been the past three days, were isolated, cut off from the Piute and its affairs. His last stop on his rounds had been at Frank Ashton's, and Ashton had been in town that day. Zack hadn't been able to swallow the story going around about it all being the work of Daycie Newkirk. He had started home at once, worried about Sam Milliron again and coming around the south end of Red Cedar so as to pass Sam's place.

He turned and stared down at Bernie's still form on the floor. "I'll get him out of here," he said. "I'll take care of Ty. Don't you worry about Sam, Nancy."

"I'm just as worried about you."

He studied her through softening, clearing eyes. How strange that he had come back to the Piute talking it for granted that relationships were the same as they had been when he went away. He had borne that hopeless love for Evalyn, actually only a nostalgic memory of the past. This woman, this Nancy, was a reality that belonged to this day, this place, to him if he had the right to claim her.

A warmth went through him and with it came his awareness that since the day they went to town together she had been the one. That was good to know when there was so much known that was not good. His brother was a murderer, he had no doubt of that now, and yet his brother was his brother, also. He didn't know what he would do now, but he wished he could tell Nancy how it would have been with them had he been able, this time, to stay on the Piute.

She had an astounding way of divining his thoughts, his feelings. Quietly, she said, "You weren't involved, Zack. I know that. But even if you were, I'd still love you. It's not just because you're a good man, but because you're you."

"I love you, too, Nancy," he said humbly. "I wanted to kill that thing on the floor for even thinking his kind of thoughts about you. But I don't know what I'm going

130

to do now. I never wanted Ty to take up with Bernie Quick, but he's my brother. No matter what he's done or is, that's a thing that was always everything to both of us. He'd leave me but come back. When he wanted to come here, I came. It started when we were kids, and that much never changed."

"My dear," Nancy said quietly, "that much was good and still is. I wish I could help you."

He shook his head. "I've got to see that neither of them does more harm, and I don't know how I'm going to do it."

She stared at Bernie, where Zack's eyes were fixed. "Aren't they the ones who ought to be where Daycie's going?"

"They're not crazy. They're spoiled, the way a good horse can be spoiled. But a man can kill an outlaw horse. Is that what I've got to do to them?"

Desperately, she said, "Ty must be on MQ waiting for him to get back. Maybe you could talk him into giving himself up since you're the only one he really cares for."

"I'll try."

He threw a pail of water over Bernie's head, reviving him. He hauled the man to his feet, took his gun, marched him out and made him mount. He looked back at Nancy just once, long and hungrily, then he swung to the saddle and the two of them rode out into the night. Bernie was still dazed, but by the time they reached the road he began to revive.

He said, "You got it all wrong, Zack. She's always hated me. She acted that way out of spite. I never laid a hand on her, honest, and I never intended to. I just sweat her a little because she always let me know she thought I was dirt."

"She thought right."

"Don't you believe a thing she said!"

"Bernie, I'd as soon put a slug in you as look at you. I know now that what's happened is why Ty wanted to come back here. But without you and your coyote mind I might have handled him and got him away before it was too late. That much is my own fault. I shut my eyes to too much. I take the blame for that."

131

"All right," Bernie said in sudden savagery, "believe what you want to believe."

"I know what I can't help knowing. You're killers, both of you."

"So what are you going to do about it?"

"That I don't know yet."

"You're a righteous son of a bitch. I never did like you."

Zack did not reply.

It was around midnight, he thought. The Piute was empty, obscured by the blazing canopy of stars, the formless air that carried vague scents of mystery and untamed nature. Yet he knew that he still loved the desert, that actually he had never been cured of the homesickness that had been so strong in him that winter on Hayfork, up on the Crooked.

He had only buried it with so many other things, and he wondered why a man had this graveyard in his mind and soul where so many things that died had to go, where ended so much that he had to kill and yet, which was the marvel, why every bit of it could be resurrected under the right circumstances. Was a life like that, a soul, itself? A man did not live in the present, which did not exist. He moved in time with only a backtrail of pleasure and pain, a foreground of bewildering complexity, and maybe somewhere beyond that mystery there was a renewed wholeness for everything.

There was a light at MQ. Ty looked angry and yet relieved when he saw who rode in.

"How did you two meet up?" he asked. He began to stare uneasily when neither Zack nor Bernie answered, when at a curt word from Zack they swung down to the porch without putting up their horses for the night. Then he saw the extra gun Zack carried, Bernie's empty holster. "What is this?" he demanded.

"Go on indoors," Zack said. His voice was brittle. They moved inside.

"You damned idiot!" Ty blazed at Bernie. "What have you pulled now?"

With a jerk of his head at Zack, Bernie said, "Ask him. He's got his side of it, and I've got mine."

"If I hadn't reached Milliron's when I did," Zack said

132

in a voice cold as blizzard wind, "he wouldn't be alive right now. I'd have killed him."

"So that's it," Ty breathed. "You sure were bent on tearing the bone out tonight, weren't you, Bernie?"

Zack answered. "And he tore it out. He admitted to Nancy that you two did the killing I've wondered about all along. That you and him are riding tonight, so it didn't matter what more you did."

"Why, he's clean out of his head."

"I am, like hell!" Bernie retorted. "How about that yarn Evalyn told the sheriff about you sleeping with her the night Ben Newkirk was killed? You forgetting Ed Larkin knows it was a lie and has probably gone to the sheriff, already?"

In a voice tense with fury, Zack said, "So that's how you got clear of that one. You're lower even than I thought."

With a quick, darting motion, Bernie slid in. He had drawn the pistol in Zack's holster before Zack, in his intent staring at Ty, realized what was happening. Bernie stepped back, smiling.

He said, "The whats and wherefores don't matter, now that I've got this in my hand. We're going, Ty, you and me. There's all that dinero up at the old cabin. We're going to get it for our stake. We'll take care of old Sam Milliron on our way north."

"Don't hold that gun on him!" Ty said savagely.

"Because you think he's your brother?" Bernie said, the gun never wavering. "Well, he ain't. The law's coming, and he would have held us, and where's the brother in that? Get some rope and tie him up. He'd stop us if he could."

Ty rocked on the balls of his feet as he stared at Bernie, then at Zack. After a moment he said, "He's right, kid. I never thought there was much chance of getting away with it, and the whole thing blew up tonight. I've got to go with him."

"I'm asking you, Ty. Don't do it."

"I should stay and hang?" A fevered light Zack had never seen there before came into Ty's eyes. "I should hang when the men who murdered my father weren't even arrested! Is that what you mean? Where's justice, damn you? Why did they get away with it? Because it

133

used to be fashionable to hang horse thieves and they thought he was one. A little mistake. Well, I righted that."

"If you're going, for God's sake leave Sam Milliron alone."

"Leave him alone?" Ty shouted. "He's the one I saved for the last. Because I wanted his guts to tighten every time one of the others died." He swung to Bernie. "If you've got ink, a pen and some paper, get 'em."

"What for?" Bernie asked.

"It'll cost you something to get a share of Kelsey's gold. We're signing over our share of MQ to Zack. He's got that coming and a lot more. He's a better man than us put together and multiplied by ten. I cost him a good future. Maybe he can find another here with us off his hands."

"I don't want that, Ty," Zack said. "All I ask is for you to give yourself up. At the very least leave Sam alone."

"You're sure gone on that girl," Bernie sneered.

"I never loved anyone as much, not even my brother. I'm asking you to give yourself up, Ty. If you don't, then somehow, I swear to God, I'll kill you."

Ty's cheeks were stiff. Then, "Get that writing material, Bernie."

"Watch him. He's made it clear what he'd do if he could."

"Do what I told you."

Zack saw from Ty's face that they were now open enemies. He wondered how many other men had seen those features that way during Ty's long absences through all the years since they went away. All at once he realized this was precisely the way Ty had looked in the moment after he had killed Loman, so long ago on the Wyoming cattle trail. Ty was a killer, and it didn't matter whether he had been born or made.

Bernie didn't trust Ty's watch on Zack. He said, "I'll trade my interest in MQ for an interest in that gold cache any time. He can have the works, for all of me. But we ain't taking any chances with him. Set down in that chair, Zack. Ty, get a rope and tie him there."

Zack sank onto the chair Bernie indicated. Ty took a look at Bernie's reckless face, shrugged and went out-

134

doors. When he returned he had a coiled catch rope. He lashed his brother there, but even then Bernie came over and checked the knots. Then Bernie got the writing material, and they sat down at the table.

Zack no longer felt anything, too much had happened in the last couple of hours for him ever to have ordinary feelings again. Hard as he tried, he couldn't keep scenes out of the lost years from flitting through his mind, the three of them hunting together, four of them, when Kelsey was alive, up in the Owyhee after wild horses. Inevitably this chain of thought drew into his mind that final night, when the ranchers of the Piute had stormed the cabin after Kelsey. For just a moment even now he could feel what Ty did, understand a part of what moved him so compellingly. There had been no justice then or afterward, and why did this moment have to be?

He knew that Bernie would never trust him again, but if he said the word Ty would break with the man. It could be himself and Ty who once again left the Piute. Somewhere there must be a place to lose themselves and live out their lives. The men who had made Ty a killer were the only ones who had died for it here. Ty bore no ill will against anybody else on the desert. He still owed Ty something, even giving up Nancy and going into hiding with him. He knew Ty would be at a loss without him, just as he would always be without Ty.

Even as these thoughts tore him, he knew it couldn't be that way. Wrong was wrong, and it was no man's privilege to take divine judgment into his own hands. The only one of the four men who had been on Red Cedar he had himself forgiven was Sam Milliron, and that because Sam had confessed and proved his regret. The others had not, and Jake Michaels had written off Kelsey's misfortune as good riddance. Yet he had not wanted to punish even them. And that difference in them had forever separated him from his brother.

The two men at the table finished their writing. Himself distrustful of Bernie, Ty read what the man had written, then nodded, satisfied. He looked at Zack.

"These papers might not be any good under the circumstances," he said. "I don't know. But the only ones who could dispute your right to MQ are me and Bernie. I won't. I'll see he never does."

"I don't want a thing, Ty, but what I asked."

"Kid," Ty said, his voice softening, "I'm sorry I can't give it to you. It was Sam Milliron out there that night yelling to Kelsey to give up and let them hang him. I heard that voice and seen his face in my dreams for years afterwards. Still do. Don't you see, I had to kill them, I've got to get him and get that out of my head. It's all I ever really wanted. You think I'm better than I am, kid. I never was any good after that night."

"Let's cut out this damned talk," Bernie said angrily. We've got a long piece to ride. We're taking his gun and running off the horses just in case he gets out of them ropes. And if it wasn't for you, Ty, do you know what I'd do instead of signing over my share of the ranch to him? I'd put a slug in his guts."

"He kept you from something you hate to give up, did he?"

"I can still go back after that filly. Maybe I will."

"No you can't," Ty said. "Because if you tried it, I'd kill you, myself."

They got together the things they meant to take, making up light blanket rolls, including a little food and plenty of ammunition. Ready, finally, Bernie looked around the shabby room with a hint of sardonic laughter in his eyes. "The old ancestral home and my birthright!" he said. "And you're welcome to 'em, Zack. The ghost of old Thurm, too."

"Get out of here," Ty said, and waited while Bernie tramped out. Then he picked up his blanket roll and hesitated. Finally he moved slowly toward the door, as though he was trying to think of something to say. But at the door he only looked back at Zack for a long moment. Then he stepped outside.

A moment later the beat of hoofs rang out.

18

For a while after Zack rode out with Bernie Quick, Nancy stood motionless, watching from the porch until distance had dissolved them, her feelings shifting like shadow play upon the mountain. Uppermost was her irrepressible gladness that at last her love for Zack had been spoken, bringing recognition to him of his own feelings. She had known it was to be since that day when she invited herself to town with him, impatient with the restrictions placed upon women.

But with her new-found joy was a deep sadness about Zack and Ty, for she could not influence the decision Zack must make or do anything to help him until he had found the way for himself. The revulsion with which Bernie had filled her whole being was still there, deeper than the clean feelings, keeping her aware that this night still held mortal danger for her father if no longer for herself.

Then a new fear came, the sure knowledge that no matter what Zack decided he might not succeed in doing it. As Ty's brother, he could not accurately weigh the viciousness of which Ty was capable, and there would be an element of love and trust that Ty would use to save himself. She knew that about Ty Maxon, just as she had always been aware of it in Bernie Quick. They were the bad eggs she had told Bernie they were and, seen objectively, Kelsey Maxon was no better. A real father would not have given his sons that kind of training if he expected them ever to live decently within the confines of human society.

She began to wonder if she should trust Zack's ability to keep Ty and Bernie from going to the Hames ranch on the Roaring Horse to kill her father. It was a long ride, but prudence began to counsel that she should take it and warn Sam, making doubly sure that he would not be murdered. She moved hurriedly back indoors, pulled off her

137

dress and stepped into her riding skirt. She pulled on boots, then donned a blouse, and wrapped a bandana about her head. She had her own pistol, which her father had given her long ago and taught her to shoot, and she got it and strapped it on. Before he left Sam had run her favorite horse into the corral, wanting her to have it handy if she was to be alone. She roped and saddled it swiftly.

She turned north on the road, knowing it was between one and two in the morning. Even with fast riding, she would not reach the Roaring Horse until well after daylight. She had no fear of the desert night, she had been out in it times unnumbered, yet there was a knotted feeling at the pit of her stomach as she struck north. This kept her more alert than she might have been otherwise, and let her see in time the two riders coming across the range from the direction of MQ.

Had there been three or just one she would not have been so terrified. Quickly she moved her horse off the road on the right side, hoping that against the dark background of the mountain she had not been seen. In a moment she was in the juniper that dropped down almost to the road. She stepped out of the saddle and went to the head of her horse to keep it quiet. She could see out through the trees, and the two horsemen had not increased their pace, were coming on steadily toward the road. Her heart began to hammer.

When they reached the road they turned north, too, and she could see beyond doubt that it was Ty and Bernie. A dual agony seered through her nerves and brain, her fear for Zack and again for her father, for they were apparently heading for the Roaring Horse. She stood frozen, hardly breathing, watching them with staring eyes. Then, for some reason, they turned right where the old road led off up the mountain. She could not guess why they had done this, knew it was not assurance that their ultimate objective was not the Roaring Horse.

She stood torn between two desires, to rush ahead to warn Sam and to go to MQ to find out what had happened to Zack. She knew Zack would not let Ty go willingly.

The decision was nearly as hard as Zack's, but she made it swiftly. These men could not reach the Roaring Horse before the night had fled, and Bot Hames was

138

there to help Sam. She had to take time to find out whether Zack needed her. She moved quietly south through the juniper then crossed the road and went driving across the open range toward MQ.

From the distance as she neared she saw lamplight in the window. It was hardly assurance that nothing had happened to Zack, yet she kept her eyes glued to it. Her noisy arrival in the ranchyard brought no one forth, and she was out of the saddle and running before the horse had stopped. The door was shut, but she burst it open, and there Zack lay on the floor, tied to a chair, unmoving.

"Oh, my darling!" she cried and dropped to her knees beside him.

A picture of what had happened flashed through her mind. She knew he had struggled to free himself and overturned the chair, and his head had struck the leg of the cast iron stove against which it lay. His mouth was open, his breathing heavy. The rope had been knotted with determination; she found a knife and cut the rope in several places, letting him roll slack and free on the floor.

As if the physical release likewise freed his brain, he groaned and opened his eyes. They were dull and vacant for a second, then came alive with surging life. He let out a groan as he shoved himself to a sit.

"I don't know how you got here," he muttered. "But thank God. I've got to stop them, Nancy."

"They went onto Red Cedar. I saw them and hid."

He nodded dazedly. "Red Cedar." His jaw tightened, and he pushed himself on to a stand. Then, dully, "Bernie won. I've got to stop them."

"Yes," she agreed. "My horse is fresh."

"I'll have to have your gun." The words were very quiet, very steady. She felt a wrenching pain, knowing the decision he had come to.

Then she handed him the gun.

The swift riding cleared his mind. From what Nancy had told him, they weren't far ahead of him. He might intercept them as they came off the mountain with Kelsey's gold. It would take them a while to dig it up. They had taken their time at MQ, had no immediate fear of pursuit. They had not counted on Nancy, and though he had no idea what had brought her it seemed inevitable that she

139

should have come to give him her horse, her gun, knowing what he had to do.

He cut the north road and at the mountain turn-off pulled up his horse. It was impossible in the darkness to determine if they had come down and moved on toward the Roaring Horse. He measured the time it had taken Nancy to reach MQ, riding like the wind, and for him to get back here, and decided they were probably on the mountain yet. But he couldn't waste time waiting here, hoping to waylay them. He would have to go on toward the cabin and come back in case he did not encounter them.

He started up the grade, bareheaded, his body without feeling but a dull sorrow in his heart. He wouldn't let himself remember how many times he had ridden this grade with Ty and Bernie. That had ended ten years ago, and this was only an echo, struck far down the reach of time. The horse kept to a good clip all the way to the top. Just as it crested over, Zack saw, far forward, a single rider coming toward him across the open ground. He pulled his horse into the juniper, staring hard across the night, bewildered by that single figure.

Bernie, he thought presently.

The man was not hurrying, so Ty for some reason must be coming along behind, Bernie riding slowly to let him catch up. But as horse and rider drew steadily closer, no follower appeared. Zack turned his horse and rode a short distance to the left, dismounted and ground-tied the mount. He went back to the trail on foot.

He stepped out of the trees, gun in hand, just as Bernie came near.

"Hold it, Bernie!" he called.

Bernie quickly pulled straight in the saddle, then all at once jerked the horse sideways and rolled over onto its side in a trick they had all practiced as boys. The spurred horse drove out along the edge of the timber. Since there was no chance of hitting more than Bernie's leg, Zack shot at the head of the running horse, on a sharp angle from behind.

Bernie jerked the animal around again, his gun out and shooting fast, Zack dropped flat. He shot again, the horse went to its knees, but Bernie managed to clear himself. As the horse went down, Bernie dropped behind it. Zack

140

rose and went running forward. Aware that he was not to be given his own time, Bernie shoved up and shot. Zack's gun spoke simultaneously. Bernie went over backward and down.

Zack stepped around the body of the horse, but the man on the ground didn't move. Sitting on his heels there a breath later, he knew it was all over for Bernie Quick. The upper saddlebag was stuffed with gold coins, and he knew the one under the horse was, also.

Mounted on his own horse, Zack rode on toward the Maxon cabin, no longer expecting to meet anybody, somehow divining that a great crisis had occurred up here. When he came to the clearing a riderless horse still stood by the ruins of the old cabin. Zack rode on and saw Ty there on the ground by the hole from which the gold had been removed. He swung down. He thought Ty was dead until he heard a low, choked voice.

"Kid—is that you?"

He dropped onto his knees, seeing the dark stain all over the front of Ty's shirt.

"He shot you?"

"Just pulled—and shot."

"But why?"

For a moment Zack thought there would never be an answer. Ty's eyes closed. His breath was so shallow the movement of his chest could hardly be seen. Then, "I was—coming back, kid. To—give myself up. I couldn't live—without you—in my life. Before, I could—always come back. This way—I never could. I'm finished but—I'm glad you got here."

"I killed him, Ty."

"I wasn't—that bad."

"No."

"Kid, I always wanted—to come back here. And I—am back."

A smile broke on Ty's face. All at once some kind of energy came into him, and he tried to push up on his elbows. But he had barely moved when he fell back, slack. Zack waited through long moments, then felt his wrist.

He looked up. Above him hung the morning star, cool, remote.

THE END

141

Chad Merriman was the pseudonym Giff Cheshire used for his first novel, *Blood On The Sun*, published by Fawcett Gold Medal in 1952. He was born in 1905 on a homestead in Cheshire, Oregon. The county was named for his grandfather who had crossed the plains in 1852 by wagon from Tennessee and the homestead was the same one his grandfather had claimed upon his arrival. Cheshire's early life was coloured by the atmosphere of the Old West, which in the first decade of the century had not yet been modified by the automobile. He attended public schools in Junction City and, following high school, enlisted in the U.S. Marine Corps and saw duty in Central America. In 1929 he came to the Portland area in Oregon and from 1929 to 1943 worked for the U.S. Corps of Engineers. By 1944, after moving to Beaverton, Oregon, he found he could make a living writing Western and North-Western short fiction for the magazine market and presently stories under the by-line Giff Cheshire began appearing in *Lariat Story Magazine*, *Dime Western* and *North-West Romances*. His short story 'Strangers in the Evening' won the Zane Grey Award in 1949. Cheshire's Western fiction was characterised from the beginning by a wider historical panorama of the frontier than just cattle ranching and frequently the settings for his later novels are in his native Oregon. *Thunder On the Mountain* (1960) focuses on Chief Joseph and the Nez Perce war, while *Wenatchee Bend* (1966) and *A Mighty Big River* (1967) are among his best-known titles. However, his Chad Merriman novels for Fawcett Gold Medal remain among his most popular works, notable for their complex characters, expert pacing, and authentic backgrounds.